Tales of the Unbreeched

A Dissertation *on the Delectable Art of Preparing a Culprit for Chastisement, with Particular Reference to the Adjustment of the Lower Clothing and Related Matters.*

By Jacqueline Ophir, *drawing on the Opinions and Recollections of her Friends, the Advocations of other Authorities, and her Own Experiences.*

Illustrated

AKS BOOKS
1996

First published 1996 by
AKS BOOKS
an imprint of
THE ALICE KERR-SUTHERLAND SOCIETY
Box 12, Hastings, East Sussex, England

Also published by AKS Books:

SWEET RETRIBUTION
THE QUEEN OF THE GROVE
THE HOUSE IN ST. JOHN'S WOOD
THE WAND OF VENUS
THE GOVERNESS COMPENDIUM
and
THE FELLOWSHIP OF THE ROD

A catalogue record for this book is available from the British Library.

ISBN 1 899861 08 4

DESIGNED AND PRINTED IN GREAT BRITAIN

DEDICATION:

To whomever it was (almost certainly female) who invented
THE BUTTON

ANATHEMA:

Upon the perpetrator (known to be male) of
THE ZIP

CONTENTS

ILLUSTRATED FIGURES BY CURTUS

AUTHOR'S NOTE

To avoid complicating the appearance of the pages that follow, I have used the chapter note (rather than footnote) system on most occasions. References to quoted passages will be found at the end of their respective chapters. Some of these occur several times, and have been abbreviated as follows:

Guide = *A Guide to the Correction of Young Gentlemen*, Delectus, 1993
SR = *Sweet Retribution*, AKS, 1994.
Fellowship = *The Fellowship of the Rod* Vol. I., AKS, 1994.
QoG = *The Queen of the Grove*, AKS, 1994.
SJW = *The House in St. John's Wood*, AKS, 1995.

All translations from works in French and German are by myself and I alone am responsible for any errors they contain.

Introduction: La Déculottage

Then down their trousers both she took.
The twins set up a squall:
"Why, Mama dear, what are you at?"
She answered: "Nothing at all."[1]

A PARTICULAR QUALITY of English is its useful ability to encapsulate in a single word—or at most two—concepts that, in other languages, cannot be expressed with anything like the same economy. In one field, however, that of physical discipline, both British and American versions of English, rich as they are, seem relatively impoverished and even clumsy compared to one great world rival, French. In a *Governess* essay some years ago[2] I commented upon the highly developed vocabulary of physical discipline available to the French nation. Some of these terms are antique; others are "argot", or regional terms which have never been universally employed even in France, and in any case are now obsolescent since in recent decades the "French Version", like nearly all others, has moved closer to the "American Version" (which is ironic if you like, since in the early 1930s it was very much the other way about). But French authors have in this century contributed a very great deal of what, in my opinion, is some of the most delightful disciplinary literature ever written, with a style—and set of obsessions—all its own. Not the least part of this appeal is the specialised vocabulary, which although it has some words which directly correspond to our own, and others that correspond in a general sense, has also an intriguing few with no precise English equivalent at all. The most notable of these, a word which occurs in one of its many variants again and again throughout French disciplinary fiction, is, in its root infinitive form, *déculotter.* It has a specific meaning: to take down the trousers; and a further implication: that physical punishment is in the offing.

In the past English has furnished two equivalents of *déculotter*. *Untruss* and particularly *unbreech* both convey most of the same sense but both are now anachronisms and would be understood by few either in England or the USA. Which is a great pity, for by allowing these elegant old words to die out we have deprived ourselves of a verbal focus on what, like the French, I have always believed to be the key procedure in any refined act of corporal discipline. In modern English, this term cannot be used at all as the subject or object of a sentence without the employment of at least four separate words; whereas *déculottage* does so, as exactly as one could wish, in a mere four syllables.

This linguistic elegance has not, in my opinion, come about by accident. The term "set of obsessions" was used above in connexion with French writing (and let us not forget French illustrative work) for valid reasons; for the French, like all other cultural groups noted for an interest in disciplinary matters, have their own particular foci of heightened interest. As one might expect, the French style of discipline is more flirtatious and delicate, more teasing, than ours. It is also more often androgynous in tone and theme, and (generally speaking) markedly gentler in style, with few of the excesses that all too often disfigure our own fiction, past and present. The characters in French *romans de la discipline* are more articulate, too; the ultra-specialised French disciplinary vocabulary playing the fullest part in dialogue as well as reportage. But if there is one stylistic component that distinguishes French disciplinary authors from all others, it is their undying fascination with the procedure they call *la déculottage*, and their identification of this non-violent act as the central dynamic of the more refined chastisements. They are by no means the only national group to do so, but they have done so more precisely and frequently than anybody else.

I share this preconception to the full, which is why *Tales of the Unbreeched* has come into being. It began, as so many ideas do, as an essay in *The Governess* (Issue XI), and, encouraged by the response from Lady Members in particular, I needed small encouragement to transform it into the slender volume you now hold; not too short, not too long—just the right length, in fact, to cover a subject which, although not perhaps in the very centre of most people's image of physical discipline, is to my mind certainly the central procedure of any such event.

ALTHOUGH THE words *déculotter* and *unbreech* both generally imply a bottom fully bared for punishment by means of a single (albeit compound) procedure, this is because both terms entered their respective languages long ago when males, for whom the term was originally couched, did not wear anything under their culottes or breeches. The lowering of a single garment therefore duly bared the bottom—*il était déculotté*.

In French-speaking countries at that time the term was exclusive to males. If a French mistress wished to punish her daughter or a maidservant on the bare bottom she had only to lift the skirts (or order them lifted), an act she called *retrousser*. Breeches or culottes did not come into it since drawers were not worn.

Only when young Frenchwomen began to wear drawers as a matter of course did *déculotter* acquire a secondary, feminine application (confusingly, French girls until recent times referred to their principal undergarment as *le pantalon*), though properly this referred only to the second stage of preparation; what took place after skirts had been *retroussés*.

For males, who had by now also acquired an undergarment, the term *la déculottage* now became (in its disciplinary sense) compound; meaning the removal of two items of clothing—trousers and underpants—seriatim. The overall purpose remained the same.

In English-speaking countries, *unbreech* followed a broadly similar course of develoment in meaning. Given that *breech* is an old word for the region of the buttocks, that *breeches* (O.E. *brychan*) were simply the garment that covered that same part of the body, and that *to breech* meant to put on a pair of breeches, *unbreech* simply meant the opposite: to remove this same garment. *Untruss*, the only other old English word even approximate in meaning to *déculotter*, strictly speaking means to unfasten or undo (Fr. *defaire*).

So it remains today. Given that the prime object is the uncovering of the culprit's bottom in order to inflict physical punishment, and allowing for a very great number of stylistic and procedural variants, the basic manœuvre remains two-stage: (a) the removal from the target area of the outer garment, and (b) a subsequent similar operation performed on the inner. The tucking-up or -aside of other items of clothing, frequently a diverting coda, comes under the heading of "tidying-up", since the main desiderata have already been achieved with (a) and (b), which together form the complete act of unbreeching or *déculottage.*

TO SOME this may seem a minor and indeed unimportant part of any physical chastisement: nevertheless I believe that it constitutes a perfect paradigm of the larger event—is indeed the "core" procedure among so many—and as such more than justifies this exegesis.

It may be allowed that many do not share this view, seeing the preparation of the culprit in this regard wholly as a means to an end, a necessary evolution to be done as quickly as possible in order not to waste time. Under their ægis the act will be performed promptly and smartly by the culprit, on the word of command. There are certainly occasions when this is an appropriate approach. Institutions are much given to drills and evolutions performed to a marching cadence; commands are likely to be abbreviated into "bites" which are more easily "barkable", and the immediate obedience of the culprit is entirely taken for granted. *Déculottage* at the hands of the punisher will be rarely seen: the only time it happens is when the culprit is under form of restraint. But overall, it is a harsh environment without much opportunity for affection and very little for redemption.

I reserve no less criticism for those who, while operating within a disciplinary environment of more feminine aspect (and therefore theoretically open to the possibilities of sensitive and artistic *déculottage*), nevertheless have never taught themselves to play upon this particular instrument as it ought to be played (or even realised that it was there to be played at all). The act of unbreeching is often done hastily, fumbled (a very bad failing), or insufficiently tailored to circumstance and personality. Opportunities are lost—or worse, not recognised. Admonitions and observations that would increase the excruciation of the culprit while harmlessly enhancing the pleasure for oneself are never formulated, or, if formulated, are said at the wrong time, or in garbled form, or in an unimpressive speaking voice.

Many of these failings can be improved with practice and a little self-preparation—while experience is the best mistress of all.

Nevertheless in my perception of the act of unbreeching as the seminal component of most refined physical chastisements, I am joined, as the reader will shortly see, by a host of writers and authorities on discipline, who, in works fictional, autobiographical and theoretical, often dwell on this particular "sub-set" of a related disciplinary event or procedure with a care and concern that to me at least suggests a temporary heightening of both awareness and tension. This may be conscious or unconscious, but more often than not there is considerably more "story value" to be extracted from a scene of *déculottage* than from the (concomitant) scene of flagellation. Here is a mid-19th century example from *The Romance of Chastisement* which is as breathtaking in its complexity as it is eccentric in literary style.

> She rose in seeming wrath, went to the wardrobe, and drew forth—even the old Cupid correctors. These she laid upon the bed, undid the brace buttons, and opened the front of his Russia ducks. Unwilling to expose him in the position in which he then stood, she did not suffer the continuations to descend more than a few inches; without removing the sustaining hand, she lectured him for some time in guarded terms such as the nature of his offence required. The lecture ended, she let fall the ducks, and led him, shuffling but nothing loath, to the stool... She now removed the ducks altogether, and made other necessary preparations....
>
> This she did, turning the boy slowly and deliberately round the while, stern necessity obliging her now to expose without reference to position. Seizing her victim by the waist and leg, she hoisted him on to the altar of her lap, arranging his position there by sundry pulls and pushes.

This vignette extends the exercise over two separate locations (the bed and the stool), and three distinct degrees of unbreeching: the ducks untrussed but held loosely in position while a lecture is delivered; the ducks allowed to slip to the heels where they form a satisfactory extempore hobble to hamper the degraded culprit's progress from one location to the other; and finally the ducks removed entirely along with any other remaining impediment to bare-bottomed chastisement.

There is an ingenuity in this passage which may fairly be called artistic: a scene of calm deliberation and racking tension far more intensely dramatic than the birching which follows. And, as the reader will see in due course, this is far from being the only example, nor is it by any means the most baroque. There is indeed a wealth of creativity and ingenuity at work here in this small act of ritual preparation and (shall we say the dreaded word?) humiliation. *La Déculottage* is a drama in its own right within the greater drama, full of symbolic meaning, coded messages, intimate warning bells and other signals; in which timing and intuition are every bit as important as determination and technique. It is a perfect encapsulation, standing not only for what is happening, but also for who the participants are. It is, or can be, a beautiful act, a miniature art-form, and it is long past high time it had a book of its own.

Jacqueline Ophir
April 1996

NOTES

1. Victorian nursery rhyme.
2. Issue IV

1: The Secret Language of Unbreeching

> "Regarding the subject of unbreeching, there are two schools of thought: either to take down the subject's trousers oneself or to oblige him to do it with his own hands. Which manner would you say was the most embarrassing for him, and, therefore, the best method?"
>
> "I believe, Reverend Mother, that the subject will find it very painful to be obliged to do it himself. But to feel the hands of his punisher adjusting his underclothes and touching his skin can be no more agreeable."
>
> "Well answered!" said the Principal, smiling. "Both methods are equally good."[1]

IN WHATEVER FORM it takes, there is acknowledged power and magic in the act of ritual unveiling.

The spell cast by the nautch-dancer (and her occidental sister, the striptease artiste) springs from the open sensuality of the dance. Teasing, exciting, frustrating, and promising by turns, it is an act of withholding that nevertheless offers the hope of ultimate fulfilment. The power resides wholly with the dancer, and it is she (or he) who decides what shall be taken off, and when, and in what manner, with nobody else having any say at all in the matter. This power may be prolonged if more garments are worn; the artful removal of each garment offering separate and different opportunities for attenuation, originality and finesse.

But when the strip-tease ends and the last garment has been removed, all power departs. She must either leave the stage or remain to fulfil the implied promise of her nakedness. Her power will not return until the next time, once more fully clothed, she begins the dance. It is therefore conditional and temporary.

Sensuality is not necessarily present in a ritual unveiling. We wrap the gifts we give each other in elaborate ways obliging the recipient to ritualise and attenuate the opening of the parcel in order not to seem rude or greedy. We veil and unveil our statues to invest them (temporarily) with mystic power; we commence our dramatic productions with a formal winding-back of curtains, and we shroud from the profane our holiest objects—except on those very special occasions when the veils are removed with a pomp and solemnity that no nautch-dancer would think of emulating.

The existence of removable veils at all is an acknowledgement of two truths: that some things are properly kept concealed at least some of the time; and that ultimate revelation is both inevitable and invested with peculiar significance.

Ritual unveiling in its disciplinary sense is also a solemn revealing of The Hidden: like the removal of an altar-screen or the annual uncasketing of a holy relic, forbidden to those without the proper authority. Like the theatre curtain, it may be a self-contained act that inaugurates or terminates a proceeding—a fundamental form of dramatic punctuation; which may be embellished and enhanced, like the play itself, by the proper deployment of the spoken word. It resembles the beautifully wrapped Christmas parcel, imposing pace and order, and is therefore also a form of discipline.

Like the striptease, its potency may be enhanced by skilful attenuation; and again taking the same model, the natures and qualities of the various veils may substantially affect the overall quality and intensity of the experience. Finally, to deny its sensuality would be absurd.

Without exception, however, power is invested, not in the Unveiled, but the Unveiler. *La déculottage disciplinaire* is above all an exercise in the use of absolute though intensely controlled moral authority: it is not at all necessary or even desirable that the Object of the exercise should be a willing participant. The event is wholly minatory, and any appearance of consent or even compliance is the result of a psychological domination established long before, and not a manifestation of the Object's own will. (That the act takes place at all, in any form or variant, is a testament to this dominance.) Here, from a 1920s French novel, is an illustration of one way in which such a hold may be established—by persuasion:

> ONE BEAUTIFUL day, my aunt was advised of the return of her Goddaughter, having finished her studies in Switzerland, Germany and England, was coming to London to seek a situation as a lady's companion or family governess. My aunt had invited her to stay until she found suitable employment.

The young lady of nineteen arrived. Not having seen her since her fifteenth year, I was agreeably surprised by her svelte beauty distinguished by regular features, a beautiful blonde head of hair, wide eyes, a well-formed and energetic mouth, and fine build with provocative curves.

The sympathetic sentiments with which I greeted the young lady were reciprocated and she asked me, the first day, to call her by her first name Denise. I performed many small tasks and services for her; and for her part, she assisted me with my French lessons—she knew that language very well.

I remember well the occasion when she exclaimed: "Oh, what a great number of faults! If I were your aunt, I should whip you, you lazy creature!" I took this remark—and others like it—for teasing and took my revenge by means of practical jokes; one time, for example, I dropped a wet sponge on the back of her neck.

She called after me: "If I catch you, I'll spank you! Rogue!" But afterwards she seemed to have forgotten her threat.

Two or three days had passed since the first incident, when at a certain moment I was leaning out of the window, looking at the business and activity of the street below. All of a sudden, I felt a sharp smack on my backside. This burning contact penetrated like a small thunderbolt. I was startled to see Denise still stooping over me. She laughed.

"What was that for?" I stammered, though without straightening up.

"Well," replied Denise, "that was for your provocative pose and also for the wet sponge."

Excited perhaps by my apparent submission, Denise took hold of the thin material of my trousers, while saying in a dry tone: "Wait! I'm going to give you a spanking. Truly you deserve one!"

"No, no," I replied. "People can see us!"

"Not at all," answered Denise "There's only a garden opposite." And immediately, I felt a series of powerful smacks falling on my surprised bottom.

"Is that warming you up?" she said. "I hope you're going to be more respectful towards me—in fact I'm sure of it. But next time, I'll take down your trousers and give it to you on your bare bottom!"

Faint with shame, I murmured: "But what if I tell my aunt?"

Immediately Denise released me. "That's horrible! I don't love you any more—go away!" She turned away, visibly offended; but I took her

> in my arms. "Don't be angry, Denise, forgive me, I won't say anything about it to my aunt." Denise looked at me with suspicious eyes. "Promise?" "I promise you, dear Denise."
>
> "Even if I take down your trousers?" she answered, after two seconds of silence. Blushing, I murmured: "No." And then, under the influence of a sensation altogether new to me, I added: "You can do everything!"...[2]

It generally constitutes a distinct stage of a longer ritual, with stages both preceding and succeeding it; yet remains intensely punitive in its own right, so nearly free of the constraints of context that under some circumstances it can even constitute the main part of the penalty, without necessity for the usual sequel. Aside from the actual infliction of stripes, it is hard to think of any other component of the main disciplinary event which fulfils this condition.

It is also one of the most flexible of all these contributing components, provided sensitivity, appropriateness and expertise are employed. Possibilities for finesse and variation are innumerable. It can be a creative act, even a loving one, involving real artistry; it may be curtailed into a single imperative compressing a series of instructions into as few syllables as possible. (This is not always an ideal approach, except with highly-trained Objects.)

The procedure may properly be executed by the Unveiler, by the Unveiled (at her command), or even (again at her order) by third parties; in careful sub-stages; in continuous sequence; or with extreme rapidity. And whatever its more immediately practical purposes may be, it can be relied upon to concentrate the mind of the Object—as no other procedure can—on what lies immediately ahead. It is an act of preparation and dedication, full of codes and signalled intention, and for many of us it lies at the heart of the disciplinary experience.

WHAT ARE THE hidden implications of the act, however it is carried out? One might begin by concluding that since nudity is the natural condition of infancy, to be denuded, partially or completely, at another's will is an essentially infantile transaction, while the denuding rôle is maternal, or quasi-maternal, as in the case of the nurserymaid or nanny. (In any case with very few exceptions the entitlement and duty to undress The Infant is the sole prerogative of the female.) A further

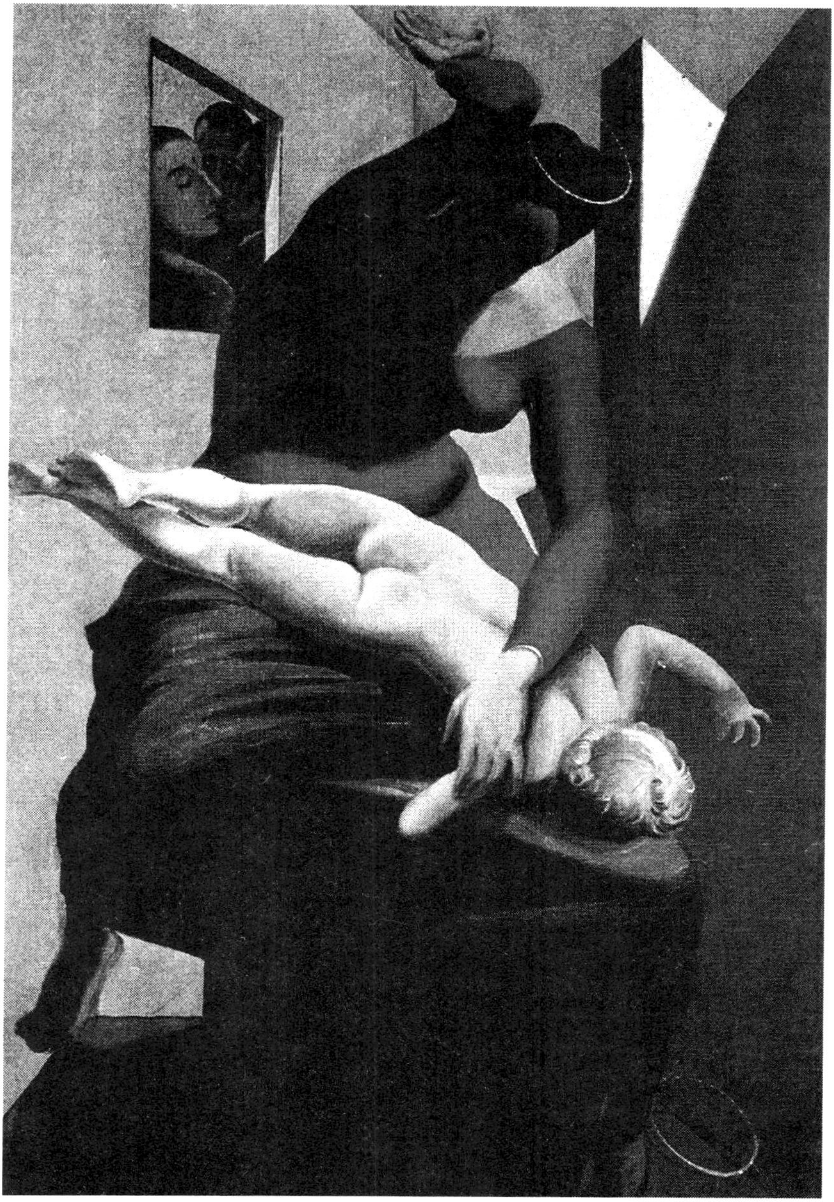

The maternal disciplinary transaction ultimately involves the nude culprit (detail from Max Ernst's The Virgin Chastises the Infant Jesus in the Presence of Three Witnesses).

implication is that any such action must be ultimately benevolent in purpose, corrective rather than vengeful. The circumstances may be intensely humiliating (because infantilising), but the punishment itself is more than likely to be relatively lenient (babies are not flogged) as a direct consequence.

But (to anticipate the objection on many readers' lips) the very harshest forms of judicial punishment—the tamarind switch in the West Indies or Africa, the rattan cane in Singapore and Malaysia—are notoriously administered on completely naked bodies. These are not delicate maternal punishments, and in no sense does the victim's nakedness represent a state of grace or innocence.

> A GREAT NUMBER of them begged to be permitted to retain their knickers at the expense of up to double their sentence of strokes. But of course, this just wasn't on, and even if it had been in our power to alter the punishment on such a request, it would have been denied, for an integral part of the punishment of the woman was her embarrassment and humiliation as she had to strip completely nude, even to removing her watch and rings once her clothes were off, before being fastened to receive her punishment.[3]

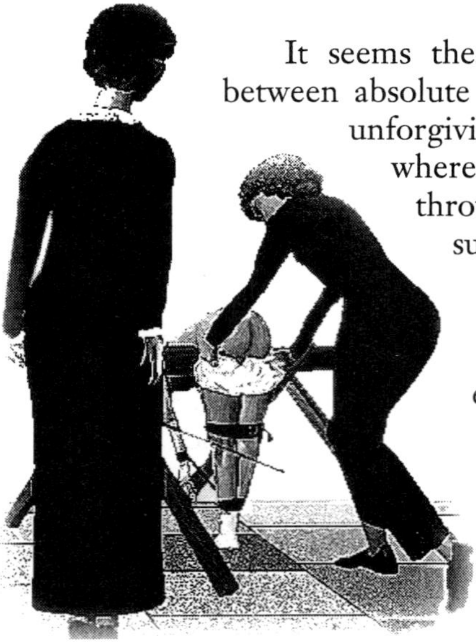

It seems there may be another correlation, between absolute nudity in a culprit and a strict, unforgiving disciplinary environment; but whereas maternal undressing rites lead, through the valley of punishment into sunlit uplands of reconciliation, the nudity enforced in judicial modes conveys a brutally different message: the crushing of all self-esteem for the foreseeable future.

But when the *déculottage* is less than total—that is, when the act of adjusting the clothing is carried out only insofar as is necessary to expose the buttocks for punishment, erring perhaps on the side of

generosity—then the message conveyed by the symbolism is already far less minatory in tone. When garments are removed altogether, they might never be given back—the "message" is that the victim has been reduced to a condition of utter servitude—but when they are pulled down, or aside, or turned out of the way, then the implicit assumption is that, once the punishment has been inflicted, they will be restored to their normal positions. Displacement is only temporary[4]. Here again we find implications of eventual reconciliation.

This "secret language of unbreeching" has other refinements to offer. To take down the culprit's pants oneself is somehow a "warmer" act (i.e. more maternal in style) than to order them taken down (which is governessy or at worst institutional). To take them down rapidly and efficiently conveys different signals (about what is to come) than trousers taken down with prolonged, even tantalising, deliberation. A brisk unbuttoning may convey, and be intended to convey, the intimation of a brisk, summary punishment to follow; and so it may often fall out. Similarly, a languid, drawn-out *déculottage* generally sends strong warnings of a prolonged and excruciating chastisement to follow in good time. In neither case are the concomitants inevitable—indeed, a canny mistress will vary the mixture from time to time in order to avoid the sin of predictability. How one performs the task is a matter of taste, style—and individual appropriateness, since circumstances are seldom identical. If the reader will forgive my quoting from my own work, here is an example of a languid *déculottage* performed in an undeniably maternal style, a seemingly gentle event that is nevertheless full of hidden menace:

ONE MORNING, NOT long afterwards, Louise was on her knees, cleaning the grate in the *salle de réception*, while the lady of the house sat in an armchair and smoked black cigarettes. She was waiting for a particular friend to call—a Madame de Trébizon. There was a mild thump and crash from the hallway. Louise got to her feet and went to the doorway to investigate. She came back and knelt down to her task again.

"What was that?" asked her employer, idly turning the pages of a ladies' journal. Louise thought she did not sound very interested, and saw no reason why she should not say—in any case, it was a light enough matter.

"Monsieur Maurice, madame," she replied. "I think he slipped when he came down the stairs. He's all right now. Not hurt at all. Nothing broken."

"Be so kind," said the widow, without looking up, "as to ask my stepson to join me." Not a note of her voice conveyed anything but mild boredom.

Louise got to her feet, went into the hall, caught the boy on his way back upstairs, and delivered her message. She saw his face change—it went oddly wooden—but she thought little of it and followed him back into the salon.

The conversation between the boy and his stepmother was conducted with Maurice standing in front of his *belle-mère*'s armchair, hands behind his back, head drooping, while she, without once looking up from the magazine so far as Louise (who had meanwhile returned to her task by the grate) could see, interrogated him about the recent mishap in a lazy, uninterested manner.

What had he been doing to cause the noise?

He had been descending the stair, *maman*, and slipped near the bottom.

At what speed had he been descending the stair?

Perhaps a little quickly, *maman*, but he had wanted—

Never mind what he wanted. He had many times been forbidden to rush about like a barbarian in the house, which was full of valuable objects. Was that not so?

Oui, maman.

"At this moment and not before," said Louise, "she put down her reading and fixed him with her gaze. She was a handsome woman with rich black hair, coiffed *à la mode*. She had cold blue eyes. She looked calmly at him, through him, almost dreamily, I thought.

"By this time I hardly had attention for the fireplace. The air was electric. I was convinced something was going to happen. And I wasn't wrong!

"The widow said: 'Tell me again what you were doing. Start from the moment you arrived at the top of the stairs and describe every single step you took from that moment. Begin.' And as she said these words—they were not said harshly—she reached languidly forward with both her long pale hands and, tugging him gently closer, turned him to his right and began to unfasten his trousers, which were high-waisted, close-fitting and knee-length, buttoned down each hip in the Spanish style; dark blue velvet, with ornamental buttons at the hem. Very expensive trousers, not the sort a boy of thirteen can readily play in. They were the only sort he was ever allowed to wear.

"He stood still and let her do it. I wanted to see his face but it was turned away from me. I could not believe this big boy would let her undress him in front of the maid without so much as a protest. But I give you my word that is what he did. And as she had bidden, he spoke throughout this procedure, his voice quivering as he tried to obey her, while all the time she was making preparations to punish him!"

For it was now plain to Louise that something of this nature was in the offing. She wondered when the mistress would notice her, tell her to go, but she did nothing of the kind. And when she had undone enough buttons on one side she rotated Maurice back to front, so that he was facing the other way, said "Continue", and began, methodically, and with the same lazy deliberation, to undo the other buttons, one by one.

Louise felt sorry for Maurice—not because she didn't think boys of his age should be spanked when they need it, but because it didn't seem to her to be such a severe offence. She could now see the boy's face quite plainly—eyes lowered, lips parted, mumbling his futile and near-inaudible relation of unimportant events.

"Continue!" said the stepmother, again, and so of course he had to ("not that she really wanted to know, you understand?" said Louise). She now turned him to face her and even while he was miserably admitting he had taken the last three stairs at a single leap, she was carefully, contemplatively, caressingly, easing the trousers, now freed from all support and restraint, down his legs, over his knees, to his calves, where they subsided into an expensive, pathetic, softly crumpled heap. The boy stood quietly in his shirt, totally passive, head drooping, and awaited events.

Louise fell silent. "Well?" asked Dorothy impatiently. "Well?" asked Mary, leaning forward tensely over her teacup.[5]

The prime object of this passage was to demonstrate self-control. The stepmother, who in reality is all eagerness to spank Maurice, nevertheless deliberately and ingeniously attenuates the preliminary *déculottage* because to control herself at this stage focuses and increases her own pleasure and anticipation. She sips the delicious wine rather than quaffing it orgiastically.

At the same time she is full of maternal consideration: for Maurice too must demonstrate self-control, and to help him remain passive and quiescent while his trousers are being delicately unbuttoned and lowered (in front of the new young maidservant by way of extra refinement), a task of which few boys in real life would be capable, she gives him something to distract his mind for the necessary half-minute; a mantra whose recital enables him to gather his courage and submit peacefully to an intensely humiliating, if not especially painful, chastisement.

Here is a *déculottage* performed by another mama favouring a very different approach—no doubt she knew her own offspring best.

FLORA DARTS across the room. That instant she is pinned by powerful arms, dragged back, and forced face downwards on the chair. In the act of kneeling, Mama whisks her skirts behind, packs them tight-drawn beneath the captive's hands, tifts and tucks-in the pendant front, and moulds the doomed posteriors to a crescent form. She then unclasps her heavy Paisley shawl, wraps it thrice around the clamorous head, secures it with a knot, and passes to the next room for a rod.

In Flora writhes and roars to be let go. Her voice sounds hollow in the triple folds; her arms are pinioned to her sides; her shoulders levelled by resistless force. One of the tutor's hands secures the skirts; the other toys around the baffling breeks, that overlap and do not break at all. Will she leave on the screen, he dares not—knows not, indeed, how—to move? Mama mediates no such treason to the stinging birch. Returning

> armed, she lays the weapon on the culprit's back, her jewelled fingers dive beneath the stays, the slit panjammies tumble wide apart and heaps of flesh appear.[6]

BUT WHAT OF the effects on the culprit him- or herself? How is the act of unbreeching perceived by those to whom it is done, both at the time and at other times? What does it mean to be subjected to this exercise? What emotions are experienced when the dreaded command is heard, or the fingers of the chastiser set to work on the garments?

Many of us perhaps will remember for ourselves but it will be useful to refresh our minds.

One might initially suppose that a culprit's first reaction would be apprehension of severe punishment, for under the circumstances of physical chastisement trousers and pants are a kind of armour; not of great efficacy, to be sure, but all there is. To be unbreeched is to be deprived of this armour and thereby to have the pain of the chastisement increased. Any dismay occasioned from this cause is therefore of a purely practical nature: it is going to hurt more than usual.

In my judgement and that of many others this is seldom the main reason why a culprit will manifest alarm when *déculottage* is either ordered or commenced. What concerns him most is the disgrace:

> ASK ANY young gentleman... whether he would rather accept a dozen strokes of the cane across the seat of his trousers, or half that number with the same garment pulled down—exposing his underwear—and it is my belief that ninety percent would choose the former option, gladly exchanging the considerable extra physical pain in a doubling of the strokes for the relatively modest component of shame

involved in lowering the trousers for punishment.

Boys are all different, but all share a common fear of being stripped for chastisement—especially by a woman. It is not the increase in pain which seems to be implied by the removal of protection (to a degree this is true but not to any great proportion, since punishers automatically compensate for clothing or the lack of it), it is the stripping itself...

The experiment may be extended into even more interesting realms by asking its subject what number of cane-strokes administered on the bare bottom he would regard as a fair equivalent of our (hypothetical) twelve over the trouser-seat or six on the drawers. He will reply: "None!". An even greater fear among guilty young gentlemen (or young ladies) is to be stripped (or required to strip) "all the way"—which of course involves the lowering of the drawers. This requirement... elevates the shame involved in a physical chastisement into excruciating regions. "On the bare" is a mighty sanction, which should not be used incontinently, but reserved for those occasions when it is not desired to hurt so much as to humiliate—particularly those crimes where the culprit's good opinion of himself has led him into error.[7]

There is little the admiring reader can add to this passage (which seems to me to define the true Terror of Unbreeching as succinctly as it has ever been done) save to note that its author clearly advocates or operates régimes where unbreeching (for punishment) is not by any means automatic: clearly some chastisements are inflicted with at least some clothing retained. This may go against some mistresses' principles, but in fact is to be recommended since it creates a new layer (or layers) in the Hierarchy of Penalties which all disciplinarians must employ. By not unbreeching (or doing so only partially) every now and again, one invests those other occasions, when what may be termed the Full Sanction is applied, with extra apprehension and gravitas.

Furthermore in our rush to attack the trouser buttons (as it were) we are in danger of overlooking what ought to be the first considered option, even for the dedicated *déculotteuse*. There are both advantages and disadvantages in allowing the trousers to be retained, and, so far as the experts are concerned, no diminution of technique.

ENSURE HE is well bent over, and that the seat of his trousers is perfectly tight. If necessary adjust this garment until the necessary drum-taut condition applies. If he is wearing a long jacket, fold back the skirt. Some Mistresses increase the ceremonial aspect by drawing out the tail of the shirt from the trousers and folding this back also, but although it must in theory diminish the protection offered by the clothing (to a tiny degree), I do not think it is worth it.[8]

There are those who maintain, and can advance physics to prove, that a thin layer of material may actually be a more efficient distributor of the shock-wave associated with a cane than the unreinforced—and highly elastic, therefore shock-absorbing—epidermis and muscle of the buttocks. A cane stroke on the bare bottom is likely to bite deeper, in other words, but the pain will also to some extent be localised. The retention of even a single garment, provided it is tight enough, can diffuse the effect of a stroke at a slight cost in concentrative power. (This, it seems to me, is at least one soundly practical reason for not unbreeching, since should one desire, for whatever reason, to inflict this particular *quality* of pain, no other method will do.)

A recognised way of ensuring the recommended tightness of the trouser-seat is for the punisher to grasp the rear of the waistband and pull the trousers *up* as tautly as possible across the seat, holding them thus stretched while the punishment is applied—an act which while demonstrably *not* unbreeching, may nevertheless be similarly defined as "intimate adjustment to lower clothing for the purposes of corporal punishment" and conveys some of the same intimate and minatory messages.

THE FIRST TIME I was about to leave the schoolroom, when my senior colleague was going to punish a schoolboy, she ordered me to remain, so that I could learn how these matters were dealt with. I submitted therefore and stayed, but I did not believe what I saw. The Mistress ordered the culprits to come forward to us at the desk; then one after the other they had to lean over the bench; and my colleague said to me:

"Watch me exactly, in order to observe the right way to do this. The boy has no right to resist—if he does, ring for a servant to hold him fast. We achieve this by severe discipline. This boy here may keep his trousers on. For this purpose we pull his jacket up—so—and take the trousers tightly in a bunch—see how I do it?—and stretch them tightly—can you see?—so that no creases remain. The boy must place his hands under his chin and may not remove them. And now that he cannot move, take the cane and thrash with full strength like this...[9]

Finally, while we are on the subject of corporal punishment administered through the protection of trousers, let us remember that, if the infliction of mere physical pain is the only object of the exercise, this may still be achieved by sheer force.

AFTER BREAKFAST on Monday morning, the boys being at cleaning and all that, Albert was summoned to the office by the chap Taft, who stood smirking in the doorway after seeing Albert inside, till told by Moloch to hook it and make sure that nobody came there till Gower had come out. The door was shut firmly. Moloch watched that it was, and Albert stood in the office facing old Moses. who was again roasting his back at the fire, Moloch being rather to the side, both hands stuck aggressively in his trouser-pockets.

"What did you want to run away from us for, you ungrateful young cub?" old Moses began at Albert. "Why shouldn't a chap run away, if 'e 'as a mind to?" Albe answered stubbornly. "What's that?" blustered old Moses. "I said why shouldn't a chap run away, why not?" Albert went on stubbornly. "That's a fine way to talk to your superintendent, a fine way!" blustered old Moses. "What in the world are boys coming to? Why, schools would soon be empty, my wilful son, if boys were all allowed to run away when they had a whim to—" "And a thundering good job if some schools were empty," went on Albert brazenly. "I don't see no use in schools, 'cept for them as're cut out for scholars," he added.

Old Moses threw back his shaggy head in utter disgust. "D'you know where you'll end up, son, if you don't change your ideas pretty quick?" he said with theatrical gravity. "Don't care anyway," muttered Albert, who, knowing what he was in for, was quite enjoying the exchanges with the old devil-dodger in the meantime. "Prison, that's where you'll soon get yourself to, son," went on old Moses at his gravest. "Well, it mayn't be a lot worse, I'm thinking, than this 'ere stinking academy for paupers," sneered Albert. "Maybe you'll change your mind, my misguided son, once you've got yourself inside," said old Moses a trifle wistfully.

Moloch shrugged his powerful shoulders impatiently, and snorted, "Sheer waste of time, sir, bandying words with this young devil. I propose we give him a good thrashing, with his trousers down, before the whole school; make a proper example of him. He's been a thumping trouble all along, and that sort're best curbed by the rod. You may remember how we dealt with the scoundrel Ellis a couple o' years ago."—"Yes indeed, and the young scoundrel ran away next day after, gave us a deal of trouble, with inquiries and what not,' muttered old Moses, "not that he didn't deserve the public chastisement we gave him, indeed the superintendent of the reformatory where he soon got sent to, you remember, told me he'd had the young scoundrel publicly flogged twice, found that was the best cure for him—but in a reformatory the case is different. That kind of public punishment is a real humiliation for the offender, as it should be, but it's rather a painful experience for the more sensitive onlookers. Of course where hardened young criminals're concerned, that objection doesn't arise. When I was visiting Newgate Jail in a religious capacity some years ago, I was invited to watch the flogging of a notorious young garroter of seventeen or eighteen, and a pretty merciless punishment it was, twenty-five lashes with a great long birch that played holy havoc with his buttocks, and I can vouch that the effect both on the young brute himself and on the collection of hardened young jail-birds brought to watch it was most wholesome and salutary, they veritably quailed at what they saw. But we cannot class all boys, I'm thankful to say, as hardened miscreants, and I would rather give this boy Gower one more chance to pull himself up than humiliate him publicly.

"So?" put in Moloch a little impatiently. "So I'll get you to give him—um, fifteen cuts—of your sharpest, understood, and with a heavy cane, in private here," went on old Moses, "and as soon as you please—"

"Let's have the beggar's shirt up, at least," snapped Moloch, "as we had Garfin's when we thrashed him for dirty habits."

"Yes, that was a very satisfactory punishment," mused old Moses, "and I gather there've been no further complaints of him in that respect."

"He's learnt his lesson, I think," said Moloch tersely. "Yes, you may take Gower's shirt up," nodded old Moses, "and arrange him as you want. I think we had Garfin touching his toes."

"That's just how we'll have this beggar, with your leave," snapped Moloch.

He then selected his cane, a lithe four to five-footer, laying it for a few moments across the office desk, a flat-topped piece of furniture to the side of the fire-place. Next he ordered Albert to loosen his belt, and smartly pulling out the chap's shirt for him, he felt coldly underneath to make sure that there was nothing between trousers and skin—they didn't supply these young paupers with underclothes, I'd better add. Then he made the chap tighten his belt, then made him bend right down and touch his toes. Moloch then smoothed the shirt down on the chap's back, and now invited old Moses to come and do his usual part, the old man gripping the chaps head between his legs, and pressing down on the chap's back with his hands, and Moloch himself exerted some pressure as well to get the seat stretched at its very tightest.

"All as you wish it?" grunted the old man.

"Pretty much so," Moloch grunted in return.

"Fifteen clean cuts, mind," said the old man.

"I know you prefer 'em clean, sir, and I'll do m'best,' said Moloch. "It's a well-shaped posterior and pretty familiar to me." This referred to the practice, after an "extra special," as punishments in excess of ten strokes were called, and they weren't frequent events, of calling the punished one into the office on the following day, and inviting him to strip and have his stripes counted—this in case he should later accuse them of giving him excessive punishment.

"Take your time, friend," said old Moses, "save the lad's soul, but don't spare his bacon."[10]

BEFORE WE MOVE to a more detailed examination of the ways in which unbreeching may be accomplished with style and efficiency, let us ask ourselves *why* we desire to carry it out—not just on this occasion, but on every occasion that we ordain it. Not why it may be good for the culprit, or justified by the needs of discipline, but why we choose to do it. For better or worse, here are a few suggestions of my own, beginning with the obvious, practical—and specious:

Because it will increase the pain felt by the culprit, all other factors remaining the same. This will spare the punisher some physical effort.

Because it will inflict humiliation upon the culprit, which adds to his punishment. The same "force-multiplier" benefits as above (the greater the shame the less need be the pain, to quote our Patroness) also apply. If the culprit's underwear is itself of an embarrassing or intimidating nature the humiliation will naturally be even more extensive.

Because we can keep visible track of the punishment, and control its accuracy and force with complete precision. This only applies to bare bottoms, obviously.

Because to unbreech a culprit reduces the chances of dissent, rebellion or absconscion to zero. Again, a practical consideration (and one which bears on non-corporal punishments as well: confiscating breeches is an excellent way of "gating" or "grounding" a culprit).

Because taking down the trousers is a necessary preliminary to a full décu-lottage, *which you have not yet ruled out.* The tacticienne's choice, referring to a particular and well-used variant in which the punishment is commenced on the seat of the knickers—on the clear understanding that even a single violation of the recognised behaviour code while under punishment will result in a pause, the completion of the full *déculottage*, and the resumption or re-commencement of the punishment on the bared bottom. (Several variations of this gambit will suggest themselves to the creative mind.)

The following reasons are, I feel, even closer to the essence:

Because to ordain and carry out any degree of unbreeching is simultaneously an exercise in lawful power and a satisfying confimation of it. Why do we take their pants down?—because they are there!

Because males in their shirt-tails, bare-bottomed or otherwise, with or without clothing around their knees or ankles, and notwithstanding whatever else may be happening to them, are usually comical, often appealing, and sometimes even quite pretty. And there is no rule that says we may not enjoy our work.

CHAPTER NOTES

1. *Cuisant Noviciat* (Paulette Vergés), Orties Blanches (Paris), 1930.
2. *Monsieur Paulette et Ses Épouses* (Jacques D'Icy [Louis Malteste]), Orties Blanches, 1929. The quoted passage is from a reader's letter (in response to an earlier volume in the same series) published as part of an appendix. This was common practice in French disciplinary literature of the period.
3. *Shades of Singapore: Judicial Caning in South Africa* by Sister Balfour (Blue Moon, 1995).
4. It might be more accurate to say that it may only be temporary. Further disciplinary value may easily and spectacularly be derived from unbreeching simply by extending this condition of dress well beyond the chastisement proper.
5. *SJW*, V.
6. *The Romance of Chastisement.*
7. *Guide.*
8. Ibid.
9. *Die Rute in Knebenheim* ["The Rod in a Boys' Home"], Hannover, 1920.
10. *The Blue Marble* (Aubrey Fowkes), Fortune Press, 1957.

2: The Mechanics of Unbreeching

It can't be helped, it must be done
So down with your breeches and out with your b–m.[1]

TO PERFORM *déculottage* upon a culprit should seldom if ever be a matter of diving into the unknown. Culprits may wear any of a dozen combinations of garments, each requiring its own "tricks of the trade" if the proper atmosphere is to obtain during its removal (which is a polite way of saying that these must be learned if a fiasco is not to be the result). Males may wear trousers, shorts, pyjamas or breeches in the course of their daily lives. I have known doublets and hose and even slave-boy tunics—and *pro tem* many varieties of female attire *[see Fig. 8, p. 69]*. Underneath these outer garments they may—probably will—wear some form of underdrawers; pants, knickers, briefs, call them what you will. These are the inner garments, and while it is not obligatory to remove them—to stop thus short of a full *déculottage*, as it were—be in no doubt that their removal provides, for the culprit, the true crisis of the procedure. But long before one reaches that stage it helps—to say the least—to know one's way about.

TROUSERS THAT fasten down the front can really only be unfastened from the front; that is, with the culprit standing in front of you. It is possible to reach around his body from the back to perform this task, but it is not easy. On the other hand, trousers that fasten at the side, or at the back, or depend entirely upon braces for support, or are elasticated, may be taken down at any stage, and for this reason are greatly to be preferred. Shirts should be tucked up, rolled up or pinned up (in which case you must have a pin handy). A shirt that slips down during punishment is no more than a minor nuisance, but the business must nonetheless pause while it is tucked up again.[2]

Here speaks the empirical expert. Even so, the scenario envisaged in the above passage rather implies a passive or at least cooperative subject. A sound knowledge of the "architecture" of clothing is even more vital if the subject is unwilling, as he is in the following case:

AT LAST, WHEN my elbows nearly touched each other, Elise fastened the cords and stood up, looking very pretty with the flush upon her smiling comely face caused by her exertions. "Now, Elise, make him kneel quite close to my knees. Put that belt round his waist, and fasten his ankles to it at the back, so that he cannot get up. Now, Master Julian," she went on when this had been done, "you are in a fit state for punishment and you shall have it. You were rude to me about those letters." Smack, smack, in my face, one on each cheek: one with the left, the other with the right hand. How those soft, lovely, dimpled hands stung! How my cheeks tingled! How I struggled in absolute helplessness to get free! "You object to a governess, to feminine domination, to petticoat-rule"—giving me two smacks at each enumeration. "I think I shall convert you. You see"—smack, smack—"you must endure it." I would not have believed two dainty little hands could have caused such pain. Kneeling at Mademoiselle's pretty feet, in close proximity to her, and seeing her graceful figure each time she raised her arms to inflict me punishment, was I own, at first, some assuagement of my pain. But at last the smacking she gave my cheeks made my head swim and I became so silly and bewildered that I was almost unconscious by the time she put the backs of her hands alternately to my lips and made me kiss them and thank her. "Oh, please undo my arms and let me get up." I longed to move about and to put my hands up to my face; but she refused. Instead, she enquired of Elise whether I had not been rude to her.

"Yes, Mademoiselle, very rude. Master Julian spoke to me most rudely when I went to his bedroom to show him the way to the breakfast room." "Very well, Elise. Out of school hours Master Julian is to be under you tomorrow and the two following days, and by that time I trust you will have made him respect you. And now, Julian, you shall be deprived of your trousers. Take a long leave of them. When you will see

Fig 1: Unbreeching from the Front

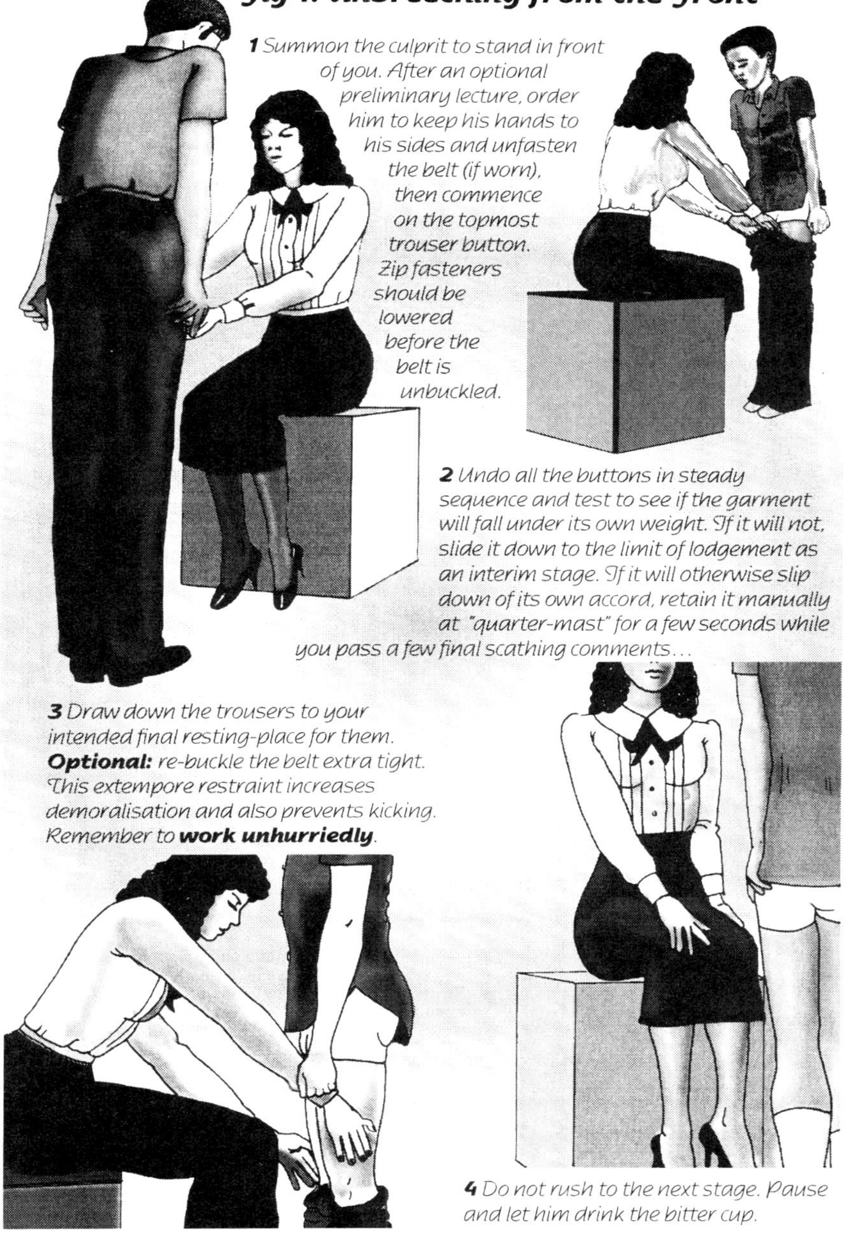

1 *Summon the culprit to stand in front of you. After an optional preliminary lecture, order him to keep his hands to his sides and unfasten the belt (if worn), then commence on the topmost trouser button. Zip fasteners should be lowered before the belt is unbuckled.*

2 *Undo all the buttons in steady sequence and test to see if the garment will fall under its own weight. If it will not, slide it down to the limit of lodgement as an interim stage. If it will otherwise slip down of its own accord, retain it manually at "quarter-mast" for a few seconds while you pass a few final scathing comments…*

3 *Draw down the trousers to your intended final resting-place for them.* **Optional:** *re-buckle the belt extra tight. This extempore restraint increases demoralisation and also prevents kicking. Remember to* ***work unhurriedly****.*

4 *Do not rush to the next stage. Pause and let him drink the bitter cup.*

them again, I do not know; they teach you all sorts of resistance and naughtiness and make you assume airs of ridiculous superiority which you do not possess. We must make a girl of you. Elise, make him stand up and take them off." "Oh, Mademoiselle! Oh, please do not before you and the girls. Oh, don't—" Elise, however, speedily unfastened the straps which kept me kneeling, but kept my elbows still confined, and busied herself in unfastening my buttons. Maidlike, she tore open all the front first, to my intense shame, and then fumbled round my waist with both hands at once, kneeling before me. I cannot describe what I felt at being close to a girl in this condition with her hands busy about me, the front of my principal garment opened and violated, and my person almost coming into actual contact with her swelling bosom as she proceeded with uncompromising promptitude and rapidity to unfasten my trousers, my governess and the three girls looking on with amusement. I myself felt like a fowl about to be roasted and was nearly stupefied with shame.[3]

These are two extremes. Here is the half-way house:

ONE, TWO, three days went by, without the dreamed-for event taking place. It seemed that Denise didn't notice my practical jokes, vainly intended to provoke her. But, the third day, on returning from school, and crossing the corridor in order to enter my room, I saw Denise's door opening just as I passed. The young lady, standing on the threshold, motioned for me to enter.

"You have continually been teasing me lately! The moment has arrived for your correction. Yesterday you slipped a horsehair brush under my bedclothes! It's the right moment. Your aunt is out until seven. Take off your jacket and let down your trousers!"

Even while I protested at this, Denise hunted in a drawer where she found, hidden under some lingerie, a short and supple birch-rod of yellow colour which was of a different texture to birch-wood, as I could tell by sight.

I removed my jacket; but embarrassment prevented me from carrying out the remainder of her command. "Must I help you?" Denise demanded and, without further ceremony, she began to unfasten my buttons. This done, she started work on the buttons at the back. I protested: "Oh, I can do it myself"—"Then hurry up!"

Then, the trousers arranged, Denise pulled me towards her. Seating herself on a chaise longue, she took me across her knees and, holding me under her left arm, tucked up my shirt.[4]

My fourth example is, alas, once again from my own œuvre:

THIS GAMBIT was all to do with the punishment of boys, and had particular relevance to the taking down of trousers. In schools which inflicted corporal punishment on the male sex, nine times out of ten the youths were, unless very young, obliged to unbutton and lower their own clothes. Schoolmistresses and -masters who did not allow this particular dignity (or extra burden) were inclined to be brisk about the unbuttoning and pulling down, the entire process, in experienced hands, taking not more than a few seconds. But Miss Newton, in the course of administering her spankings, had evolved a third method.

Her method was to summon the culprit to her side, and then herself to unbutton the trousers or breeches with a calculating slowness, all the while holding the pupil's gaze and speaking to him of his fault. In those days boys' trousers were buttoned at the sides, like girls' are today, so there was no danger of Miss Newton's fingers accidentally touching something untoward. A crooked forefinger in the waistband would pull the unhappy or defiant youth to her side, and then, one by one, the large flat buttons would be undone, all to the accompaniment of a relentless and evocative panegyric on his immediate fault, weakness of character, immediate destiny and her own sorrow, delivered in a steady tone. For example:—

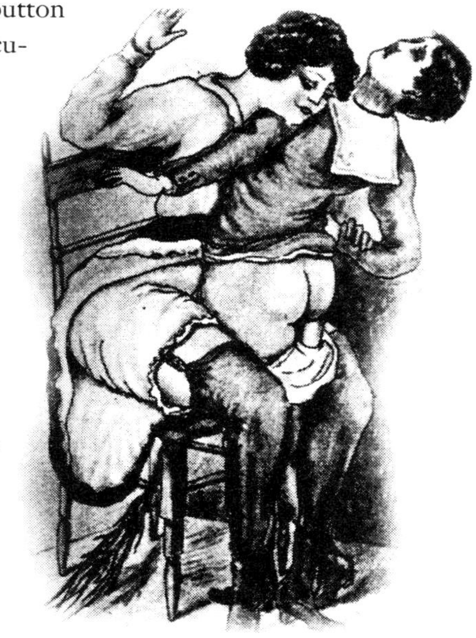

"Now Jonathan. You know perfectly well what I promised you the very next time you misbehaved." (Pop.) "I told you, did I not, that I should be obliged" (pop) "to put down your trousers before the class"

(pop) “and put you over my knee like the silly little boy you are” (pop). “No—take your hand away, sir! And do not struggle. Big boys are allowed to lower their own trousers“ (pop), “but you are not yet a big boy, otherwise you would not behave so badly, obliging me to” (pop) “unfasten your buttons and pull them down” (slither). “There, sir! Now I trust you feel ashamed in your shirt-tails before the girls! Place yourself across my knee at once!”

And so on. Thus Miss Sophie Newton.[5]

The moral to be drawn from all four passages taken in conjunction is this: dictate circumstances where you can, adapt where you cannot. Miss Kerr-Sutherland never dreams of an environment where she is not instantly obeyed and her recommendations reflect this; but the maid who unbreeches Master Julian in *Gynecocracy* is no less expert than she in the attributes of male costume, and even though she is obliged (this once) to work under pressure is entirely successful. Denise, on the other hand, proves herself above all adaptable. She gives

Fig. 2: Unbreeching from the Rear

Rarely employed in its own right, this is nevertheless a valuable technique and should be practised since it is the key to nearly all other modes (especially over-the-knee unbreechings) where fingers must be able to unbutton sight unseen. Note the obediently-maintained “unbreeching posture”.

an order: when it is not obeyed quickly enough (perhaps it was not really possible to do so) she changes her plan without hesitation and concludes the unbreeching with her own hands and to her own satisfaction. Finally, Sophie Newton knows what she wants and achieves it flawlessly every time with very little variation ever employed.

One might also note in passing that in three of the examples the adroit use of spoken words subtly increases the natural tension of the event and exacerbated the culprit's sensibilities (see Chap. 4).

It is the ease, convenience and dispatch—not to mention the line-of-sight approach—of the Standing Frontal Method of Unbreeching *[Fig. 1]* that make it easily the most favoured of all. Many Mistresses extract considerable extra *frisson* from the culprit's demeanour during this operation. There are culprits who look down aghast, those whose fingers feebly twitch in hastily-aborted obstructing manœuvres, those who stand rigid staring straight ahead, or who wriggle half-heartedly and protest verbally (but in no other way).

What the culprit *should* do during this time is what you wish him to do—and nothing else. One can solve all problems by means of a recognised "unbreeching posture". This can be a simple variant of the "attention" or "at ease" positions, with hands at the sides, folded behind the back or linked behind the head. It is also to be recommended because a properly upright, attentive posture presents belt and buttons at precisely the correct condition of slackness for unfastening. Stooping forwards (i.e. in dismay) or recoiling backwards (for the same reason) can cause these vital appendages to vanish into crevices or tighten, thus making them harder to deal with.

To return to Miss Kerr-Sutherland's original point concerning trousers that button down the front. Is is true as she claims that they may only be unfastened from the front? If so, this would sadly limit the modes of unbreeching available to the creative *fesseuse.*

However, it seems that our formidable Patroness may for once be in error. Firstly, there is the "reversed" mode *[Fig. 2]*. a variant which is not used often (yet is considerably disconcerting when it is!) but should be prac tised now and again because it is the "key" to so many other unbreeching postures. The second example, illustrating a different approach, is taken from a literary source and supposedly based on a real-life event.

Two adolescent boys—one of whom is the narrator—have been

caught involved in intimate mutual examination, by a young woman who is their teacher and tennis coach combined:

> ALL OF A SUDDEN, the door opens before us…it is her. With her rubber-soled tennis shoes we haven't heard her coming.
>
> At the first glance, she sees everything…
>
> 
>
> She glares at us, stupefied with indignation.
>
> We rebutton ourselves hastily.
>
> With one leap she is upon us. Roughly grabbing Gabriel by the arm, she wrenches him off his chair. She marches him to the middle of the room, into the free space between the desk and the three tables. There, pressing the nape of his neck firmly with her right hand, she bends him forwards… she presses more, to double him over. She then lifts one of her great legs to bestride him between her thighs.
>
> In vain the unfortunate one scrabbles with his feet, in vain his humiliated hands clutch at Mademoiselle's ankles; he struggles as much as he can. She, with a sure hand, unfastens the buttons of his braces, behind and in front, up and down, to left and right… Using both hands underneath, she then goes in search of the buckle of his trouser-belt, unfastens it, and then, with the fingers of her right hand, unfastens the three trouser-buttons in rapid succession. She takes down the trousers…[6]

Once more the success of the manœuvre argues a punitrix who "knows her way around" the intricacies of male clothing. To unbutton in this way, sight unseen, relying on memory and sense of touch, is an operation calling for considerable skill—and confidence. A culprit face down and possibly bent in the middle is not easy to deal with unless one knows just where to place one's fingers and how to manipulate them. Buttons may be under pressure and may not yield easily to a ladylike touch. Be firm if necessary, and never mind the buttons that fly away! They will be a subsequent problem for the culprit, but that is as it should be.

Even with its special difficulties the face-down position *[Fig. 3]* offers several attractions—first and foremost of these being that of course it corresponds to the across-the-knee posture that one returns to again and again in physical punishment. When culprits are across the knee they are also face down, and almost always their clothing is further obstructed by the pressure of their weight on your lap. One must either "tunnel" one's way in search of buttons and zips, or reduce the pressure and improve access by lifting up the culprit's midriff to a sufficient degree. A simple command will achieve this: if for some reason it does not, spreading your own legs temporarily wider apart will bring the target zone into "free space" where it may be attacked more easily. Once the fastenings have been attended to, bring your knees together again and draw the trousers down as far as you wish.

To be unbreeched by main force in this infantile way is an excruciating experience for the culprit, and an excellent mental *preparatif* for what follows. Let us return to the earlier incident of French provenance for another example. Gabriel has had his "fessée", and now it is the narrator's turn.

WHAT IS SHE doing? What is she preparing for me? She places a chair in the middle of the open space, facing one of the windows. Then she seizes me by the wrist. Docilely, I stand up. She seats herself, laying me across her knees. What's happening? Isn't she going to hold me like she did Gabriel? No, she is going to spank me *à la maman*.

She's going to take my trousers down like she did Gabriel's. I turn my head towards him. He is kneeling on the old-gold velour cushion beside the bench. The clear light from outside illuminates the red bottom of which I have a three-quarters view.

I am dressed like him in an unbleached drill two-piece of trousers and martingale jacket, without a pullover. She is no more disconcerted with me than with him. She knows how to unbreech a boy! And considering that in this position it's not so easy to unbutton me, she does it well.

My fly-buttons are the first to go. She lifts me, and turns me a little to pass her hand underneath. I find myself helping her, turning myself by my own efforts...

But is she going to notice how much this excites that which is still excited from earlier on? Oh, how I shall be ashamed! No, she's noticed nothing, even though I feel the tips of her long fingers brush against me when they fumble the opening my trousers in search of the third button.

It's done—I am untrussed. She pulls my trousers down below my bottom. Underneath me, my underpants are retained by the weight of my body against hers. But— how well she does it!—she lifts me up, and pulls

Fig. 3: Unbreeching Across the Knees

them down to my shins. She can now see all of me—my bottom, my thighs, everything. She pulls up my short shirt. Under her eyes I am naked from my shoulders to my shins; nevertheless she pushes my jacket and shirt as high as she can.[7]

And to prove that this is truly an international subject, here is a supportive example of the same basic manœuvre, this time from Austria. In this case the culprit is that much easier item to deal with—a girl. The chief punitrix is a nun, and her assistant—the narrator—is a young woman teacher. (The disconcerting change of tense towards the end is, I suspect, the result of over-excitement on the part of the author.)

IN THE COURSE of the lesson she tested a girl of around fourteen years and a half—her name was Annette—and received correct and proper answers. Marie-Therese then tested another girl and during the testing Annette lost her pencil and bent over to pick it up. During this movement her skirt tautened over the cheek of her bottom to such a degree that we could exactly discern the outline of her arched buttock. Marie-Therese darted a significant look at me which caused the blood to rush to my cheeks. Then she looked again at the two tempting rotundities which swelled toward us... the deep valley between stood out against them, ravishingly...

It would have to be Annette!

Marie-Therese let a little time go by, then she called upon Annette once more. The little beauty stood up and answered impudently, "But I've already been tested once." Thereupon the teacher replied: "What are you saying? You dare to answer your teacher in such a way? I'll teach you something else, you saucy child. After the lesson, you're coming with me. Understand?" Annette—"Oh, Madame, I didn't mean it that way, I didn't mean to be saucy. I just thought that you had forgotten." Marie-Therese: "What I said still stands; follow me after the lesson."

Annette began to cry—after all, she knew what the teacher's order meant. It was not the first time that she had to pay a visit to the punishment chamber.

When the bell rang after the close of the lesson, the girls scampered joyfully out of the classroom to the playground. Only Annette remained behind. She cried without letup and begged for forgiveness. Marie-Therese was pitiless and answered that an infraction like hers was unforgivable and that she must be prepared for a very strict punishment. "Now you follow us," she concluded, as she took Annette by the hand.

We led Annette, howling, to the punishment chamber. Marie-Therese ordered her to wait, took a supple birch rod out of the closet and laid it on a chair, so that Annette saw it in full view.

Annette stood in the middle of the room, pressing her tear-soaked handkerchief against her eyes and shaking with sobs from head to foot. She had already experienced many birchings here. Her bottom is of a beautiful corpulence, almost like a fully developed woman's bottom with firm, swelling, soft, but nevertheless very sensitive buttocks. She is ridden with shame when the moment arrives to unbutton her drawers and bare her bottom.

Marie-Therese had decided beforehand that she herself wanted to unbutton Annette's drawers on this occasion. Therefore she ordered her to lie face downward on the punishment bench. Annette understood that any pleas for mercy were in vain; she adjusted to the inevitable, crying, and did as she was ordered. When she lay stretched out on her belly, Marie-Therese firmly fastened the strap around her waist. Then she raised the girl's dress high—she was wearing short drawers, made of a thin cambric with pretty lace edges, that reached down to the middle of her thigh. The drawers were so tight that the buttocks were imprinted. Between the drawers and her stockings could be seen a piece of her bare thighs, which shone a beautiful white.

Marie-Therese bends over the fettered body and her hands vanish under the clothes toward the waistband. They are searching for the buttons of the drawers, which are buttoned on both sides. ...Annette implores forgiveness when she feels the ferreting hands, and makes desperate efforts to mollify the teacher at the last moment. After all it is only now that she realises that the bottom-warming is as certain as the Amen at the end of a prayer.

Silently Marie-Therese unbuttons the back flap of the drawers, pulls them down and a piece of the naked thigh appears between the flap and the chemise, which barely covers the bottom. Marie-Therese lifts the chemise, solemnly and slowly, and reveals Annette's bare buttocks which, white as snow and soft as velvet, lightly shiver for shame.

The nun reaches for the rod. All my thoughts are with her...[8]

Here, apart from any other differences, a different set of clothing (worn by the culprit, or in this case, victim) transforms the nature of the *déculottage* into a superficially different event. There are no trousers to be taken down, no buttony complication, only a dress to be turned back. The drawers are more complex than a male's of the same period might be: the text suggests that these are of the back-flap rather than back-slit or "closed" (no aperture at all) variety. These had buttons at the sides which, when undone, allowed a "trap-door" to lower: the main part of the garment remained *in situ*. It is not clear in the quoted example whether the birching was inflicted on the revealed square of bottom, or whether the drawers were indeed fully unlatched and pulled down, revealing also the thigh (a source of shame to young females of the period not greatly less than that associated with the buttocks). Either way, it is clear that the nature of the clothing allowed more than one procedural option to those who punished young ladies corporeally during this period (c.1910). Finally the excited and attenuated lifting of the chemise—a sartorial item not present in males' clothing—clearly constitutes the real "final veil".

This should remind us that even small items of clothing difference may substantially alter the unbreeching procedure, or, if unanticipated, pose problems for the novice. We have already noted the difference (both æsthetic and practical) between buttons and zip fasteners. Before we move on to the styles of trousering which make life a lot easier—elasticated waists—it is worth remembering that one particular male appurtenance, these days less commonly encountered than in former days (though in my view male elegance has correspondingly declined), actually makes life harder for the *déculotteuse*. I speak of braces, which Americans call suspenders; items of intrinsic ludicrousness which nevertheless serve a valuable sartorial purpose, and may even prove of unanticipated value in disciplinary contexts. Properly adjusted, and provided they remain invisible, these items can make a valuable contribution to the "sit" of a pair of trousers: while worn but there is no denying that as an additional garment they constitute a further task for the punisher proposing to take these same trousers down in order to inflict physical chastisement upon their owner. Author Louise Malatesta has clearly bent her thought to this particular tactical issue:

> THERE IS NO special ritual. While we eat in silence, Hannelore consults her notebook. She stands on the dais, beside a large wooden chair with

no arms. With her are two maids—the Russian and the Third French maid, the one with the short, straight, light-brown hair, the vaguely mustelid profile and the slightly protruding front teeth. She is devoted to Hannelore, though not popular with the other maids. But she has beautiful long hands and clever, delicate fingers. She is the best seamstress in the house and does all the *petit point*, but the Third French maid is especially valued by Hannelore because she untrusses more completely, more rapidly and yet more beautifully than anybody else in the Household. She is said to have received her training in the convent school where she once taught needlework.

Hannelore consults her notebook, while those of us whose mouths are not dry with terror eat our oatmeal. Needless to say, most of those "about to die" know in advance—to know in advance is a fair part of the punishment. But there are others who will suspect nothing until they are called-up. Then they go pale with shock and it has even been known for bowls to be overturned.

Summoned, the culprit will leave his or her place and go to the dais. The events that follow are of a rigid pattern—long ago Hannelore evolved this method and she never deviates from it. The offence is named. The sentence is pronounced. Then the Russian sits with her legs about a foot apart. The culprit bends forward with arms folded behind the back. The Russian grips the lowered head between her knees, and leans forward to secure the arms. The culprit is now anchored in this posture (provided the knees do not give way) until released. The bottom is facing directly towards the centre of the room—everybody has a clear view, though in theory we are supposed to continue eating.

So far, preparation of the culprit has taken about five seconds—this is not a lushly formal flogging like those administered in the evening by my lady, and briskness is the order of the day. The Third French maid now trips forward, with her hateful pursed smile, and proceeds to untruss the culprit from waist to knees. If a girl, she turns back pinafore, frock and petticoat in a moment—whisk! it's done: folded in a trice and the gather tucked under the culprit's arms, so that she is effectively made to hold up her own clothes for punishment. With trousers or breeches her speed and skill are even more remarkable. Commanded to untruss, a male will often dawdle futilely, as if procrastination were any way to make friends at such a dire moment. At other times, especially when terrified, he is likely to be exceedingly quick. But if he is quick, and especially if he is terrified, he will make a clumsy job of it; the trousers will be left to sag in an untidy heap around his shins, or to dangle foolishly from a rope of braces (as if simply lowering the trousers were the only point of the exercise!). The shirt-tail will probably not be tucked up at all, and the most important stage, the pulling down of the underpants, will be accomplished hastily and gracelessly. And even so, he will not have been as quick, or as complete, as the Third French maid, who works faster than anybody when this is required and still creates more pleasing visual arrangements.

If braces are worn she does not content herself with undoing the back buttons and letting the braces slip up the back until they reach the neck—this is what is normally done when braces are worn, and a very bedraggled appearance it presents. She always unfastens the front ones, and first, so that the braces may be removed and laid aside (unless they are required for impromptu restraint, in which case they can be wound tightly around the knees and lower legs to form an effective pinion). From the point of view of the punisher, this has two advantages: it lowers the trousers all the way to the ankles, and it increases the time taken redressing, both of which increase the shame and humiliation.

So far she will have taken about six seconds. Rolling the shirt-tail and tucking it up under the jacket or pullover takes another second.

Her way with underpants is equally deft and original:

There remains only one stage, which is the same for both genders: the taking down of the pants. Unlike almost everybody else, the Third French maid performs this task by pinching the leg-hems between thumbs and forefingers and sliding the entire garment smoothly downwards in a single, controlled movement. It seems quick, this final unveiling, if you watch it being done to others; excruciatingly slow and strangely disconcerting, if it is being done to you.

A moment to tidy the rearranged garments, and then she steps aside, with a small bow to Hannelore, who invariably bestows a cold, gracious smile on her favourite. The whole business will have taken not more than ten seconds from start to finish.[9]

From the absence of any mention of unbuttoning, one may conclude that these undergarments were of the elastic-waisted variety.[10]

This method of securing clothing to the body—first developed for children's knickers over a century ago but for many years now associated not only with the underwear of both sexes and all age-groups, but also with many informal or sporting outer garments—is for many women a *déculotteuse*'s delight, since it enormously simplifies the process of pulling down any garment thus secured to the waist (though conservatives such as myself might wistfully regret the easing of a task which, if complicated, was at least concomitantly pleasurable—and attenuable). Miss Malatesta's Third French Maid was certainly original in her way of doing this since for most of us it is the waistband which leads the way downwards, so to speak, and the rest of the garment which follows in its wake.

In passing, here are my own thoughts on braces. There is no reason why they should inhibit any standard mode of unbreeching. To a great extent this will be defined by the posture chosen for punishment (and therefore preparation): if face-down, then unfasten the rear brace only and allow the garment to slide up behind the neck (or over the head if no jacket is worn) as you draw the trousers down. These will descend only to knee-height but that is adequate for your purpose. If you have decided to unbreech from the front, then unfasten the two front braces first of all, before opening the trouser buttons, and when you have concluded seize the loose portion of the braces in the small of the back and draw the garment all the way backwards across the shoulders (this will work even if a jacket is worn). Lower the trousers to the heels. Finally, use the two tails, as Miss Malatesta recommends, to impose an *ad hoc* restraint on the lower limbs—one may in fact knot a pair of fallen trousers into place around the ankles so securely that it can take a newly-chastised culprit several minutes to untangle the mess and reclothe himself, during which time he will remain at a severe psychological disadvantage!

Once one has gained confidence in one's ability to deal with the usual set of buttons or zip-fasteners (ugh!) at nearly any angle of approach, visible or sight unseen, many other postures and concomitant modes of unbreeching become available. A frequently used method is to hold the culprit bent under one arm while you unbreech him—this time not only from an indirect angle, but upside-down! *[Fig. 5.]* The difficulties are nevertheless not so great as with this same task performed across the knee, and in any case if the bending posture makes unbuttoning difficult the culprit can always be made temporarily to relax it. Perhaps one reason why it is so often employed is perhaps it represents the most rapid and unfussy way to seize and prepare a culprit.

> "MY DEAR friend," says Madame Duhoux, "I have adopted the system of my own mother, and the experience I have had with my own children has been admirable. My little boy is ten, my daughter is twelve, both are frequently whipped and know that they will be if they require it. Have you ever whipped your boy?"
>
> "Sometimes with my hand. These days I don't dare..."
>
> "Why? Children are never too big to have good principles inculcated. My daughter of twelve is already well-developed; she is whipped just the same and will continue to be. In England, I have heard that a young

woman is punishable in this way until she is married. Too big! On the contrary, it is at the moment when young rascals begin to learn to be men, that it is important to remind them that they are still only children. They must learn this in the good old-fashoned way. Too big! On the contrary, their age makes them even more culpable, to the point where it can only have disagreeable consequences. One must simply skin their bottoms a little..."

"Oh my God!"

"Nonsense! It was done to me many times, even though I have a fair skin. There's nothing wrong about it. Like the song says, the skin of the bottom recovers quickly. You see, one must whip seriously or not at all. Therefore, do not hesitate, take a birch-rod or a good martinet, advise the young gentleman of the correction he is going to receive and do not hesitate for any reason. That said, take down his trousers in the grand style and whip his backside!"

"Oh, I don't dare!"

"Good Lord! Don't worry about his shouts. After all, you whip him so that he can feel it, don't you? Anyway, children always exaggerate. Sensibility is out of place: whip, whip hard!"

"I don't think I'm strong enough."

"Then call in the house-maid to help you. To be whipped in front of the maid is judged the epitome of shameful chastisement. Think about it! To think one-self a man and then, in front of the maid, to have one's bottom bared and whipped like a naughty little boy! My maid has permission to whip my little Jacques when he isn't good, and she does so

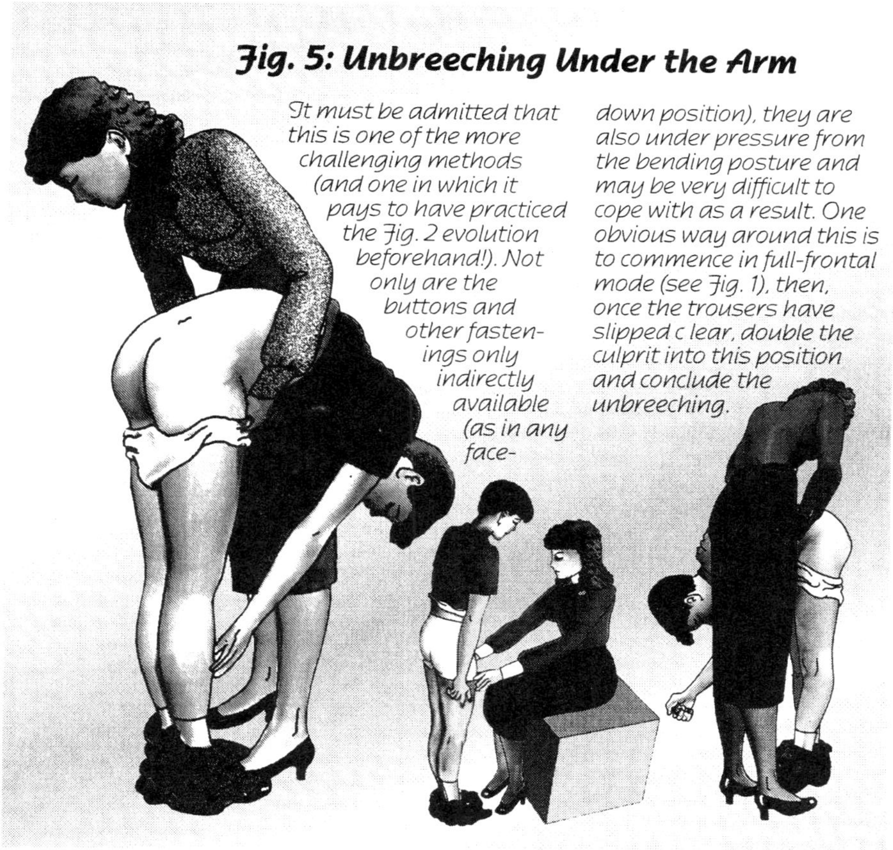

sometimes, don't you Rosalie?" she said to the housemaid who had just come in to find something.

"Certainly, Madame," answered this woman, who was big and strong and around thirty-five years of age.

"And you do it well, Rosalie," conceded Madame Duhoux. "The little rascal doesn't boast of it either. The first time, he complained to me, but since I have never taken his whines into consideration, I rejected his complaint. It is true that the first time Rosalie corrected him with my permission. You remember the first time?"

"Yes, Madame" answered the big woman, with a certain complacency. "It was a day when he was home from school and playing me all sorts of turns and tricks..."

"To show off before his friends," agreed Madame Duhoux. "So I decided, in order to humiliate him, that he should be whipped by yourself."

"This I did at once. I took him under my arm, took down his trousers and, with a martinet taken from the hook in the kitchen, I gave him a good hiding...

"Generally he is quite submissive. When he hasn't been good, I say to him: 'Master Jacques, if your mother was here, what would she do? Tell me.' With some hesitation, he replies: 'She would undo my trousers...' 'And then?' 'She would whip me.' 'Well, Master Jacques, I am in her place...'"[11]

Another example makes clear that this method of unbreeching—and punishing—holds no terrors for any competent disciplinarian determined on executing justice in one of the most summary ways available to her:

THE BOY HAD answered his mother back. She was in the yard, and became very angry. It was obvious he was going to get a terrible punishment!

His mother dragged him into the house, into the dining room, where we were talking. She held him under her arm and took his trousers down in no time at all. She really did it quickly!

And then she spanked him! How she spanked him! But she didn't hurry in the least...[12]

The close relation of the under-the-arm posture, where the culprit is held, not under the arm, but between the thighs or knees, is no less effective and far more intimidatory—and secure. We have noted this variation already (see p. ##, ##), but here, for good measure, is another example taken at a slower tempo:

"YOU HAVE COMPELLED me to use violence to make you obey, Peter," she remarked, "consequently, you will be triply whipped!"

Fig. 6: Unbreeching While Kneeling (or Bending)

Here is another unbreeching posture which while yielding excellent psychological intimidatory results also furnishes difficulties, largely for the same reasons attached to Fig. 5. The bent-over posture, allied to the indirect approach to the buttons, can obstruct the best intentions. The remedy is also the same: begin the unbreeching before the full posture is assumed. Once the pressure has slackened somewhat, press his face down and continue at your leisure. The only alternative is to order a self-unbreeching before the culprit "assumes the position."

"Aunt, dear little darling Aunt!... Pity!... I shall obey you! Oh I am going to die of shame!"

"If you do not submit without a murmur, Peter, I shall call Dorothée! This is my last ultimatum!... " I remained motionless before her on my knees, weeping quietly. Then she slowly lifted up her skirt, pushed it back on her lap, but not before she had taken good care to see that her petticoat was decently lowered. Then on this petticoat, hollow between the knees, she drew my face down and gripped my head solidly between her powerful thighs. In a moment I felt her skirt descending on me and I found myself, so to speak, isolated from the world, in a warm obscurity saturated with the seductive perfumes she knew so well how to use.

You cannot imagine the mad thoughts—the senseless desires which burned in my brain! No! That is impossible! And the shame of it, how it maddened me! Never in my life had I been submitted to any similar humiliation!... And it was still worse when I felt the hands of my feminine executioner groping around my loins, searching the buttons of my trousers, unhooking my belt, lowering my breeches on my garters and, performing the same operation for my drawers, turning back my shirt on my loins and touching my flesh before beginning to flay it! Just so the ancient priests did: when selecting a sheep worthy of sacrifice, they appraised its quality as an offering first before they slit its throat.

Across the thin material of her skirt, I could hear the voice of cousin Gretha lecturing and advising me to receive in humility and contrition the severe whipping she was going to inflict. Then suddenly a hard burning slap fell on my right hemisphere, then another on the left, then another, and still another! And the blows fell in a methodical regularity while from under the skirt of my disciplinarian rose the plaintive concert of my lamentations... [13]

CHAPTER NOTES

1. Schoolboy doggerel, late 19th cent., quoted in *Portait of the Artist as a Young Man* by James Joyce.
2. *Guide.*
3 *Gynecocracy* (H. Stanislas de Rhodes), London, 1896.
4. *Monsieur Paulette.*
5. *Fellowship*
6. *Les Mains Chéries* (Jacques D'Icy), Orties Blanches, 1920.
7. Ibid.
8. *Confessions & Experiences* (Edith Cadiveç), Grove, 1969 (first published 1930 in German)
9. *Château Soumission* (Louise Malatesta)), AKS, 1996.
10. Old-fashioned garments may be buttoned or tied with a drawstring, which requires a virtual repetition of the operation performed beforehand on the outer garment.
12. "Madame Duhoux's System", from *Confessions et Recits*, Paris, 1923.
12. *Paulette Trahiée* ("Paulette Betrayed"), Orties Blanches, 1929.
13. "Discipline at Parame" from *Painful Pleasures*, 1931, Gargoyle, New York.

3: Under Orders

Mercy were weakness, liars have their part,
Scripture declares, in everlasting smart.
Only the giver absolution grants,
This law I execute.
Let down your pants.[1]

ALTHOUGH THIS book's main area of concentration is undoubtedly centred around manual unbreeching—by which I mean the operation carried out in some fashion by the mistress—it cannot be denied, indeed is a vitally important fact, that a great number of these disciplinary unveilings will be executed by the culprit himself at the order of whoever is to administer the correction. "Take down your trousers!" is perhaps the commonest phrase ever uttered in a punishment salon.

Although I am no automatic advocate of this method, preferring to perform the operation myself whenever it is convenient, I freely admit that as a mode of initiating *la déculottage* it has certain advantages. It is labour-saving; and it allows one to make use of one of the undeniable Phrases of Power. More interestingly—and complicatedly—it is a command which is seldom uttered unless in absolute expectation of being obeyed, while at the same time its very issuance frequently guarantees obedience! Just as the Hooded Cobra is said to be hypnotised by the weaving approach of the mongoose—and the rabbit by the snake's undulating advance—so human males are seemingly transfixed by the totemic power of this phrase (or its many close relatives) and are compelled to comply, usually without the slightest demur.

IT WAS CLOSE upon four o'clock, at which hour we always broke up for a run in the garden for an hour... I had done nothing with my task—Miss

Evelyn looked grave.

"Mary and Eliza, you may go out, Charles will remain here."

My sisters, simply imagining that I was kept in to finish my lessons, ran into the garden. Miss Evelyn turned the key in the door, opened a cupboard and withdrew a birch rod neatly tied up with blue ribbons. Now my blood coursed through my veins, and my fingers trembled so that I could hardly hold my pencil.

"Put down your slate, Charles, and come to me."

I obeyed, and stood before my beautiful governess, with a strange commixture of fear and desire.

"Unfasten your braces and pull down your trousers."

I commenced doing this, though but very slowly. Angry at my delay her delicate fingers speedily accomplished the work. My trousers fell to my feet.[2]

The above example being from a domestic context, the next is judicial: but even though the *déculottage* is left to others, the response is equally submissive:

I SELECT THE nearest of the two matt-black ferrules and swish it through the air. I take the tip in my left hand and test the flex. I swish it again. Then I lay it down and select the other. In fact, I could detect nothing wrong with the first cane but it's as well, now and again, to assume a mantle of perfectionism.

The first boy—the scared one—is brought in, wearing only his underpants, as per regulation for males. He blinks at the cane, and drops his gaze in obvious shame when he sees the three women waiting to chastise him. He makes no fuss, obediently walking forwards to the "donkey" and waiting submissively while Liz adjusts the height of the bar and Tess fastens his knees to the centrepost. Then he takes a deep breath and bends forward.

"Lower!" says Tess, in a sharp tone. He bends lower. "Lower!" she says again. "I can't!" he whispers, but all the same he manages that extra inch. His wrists are fastened to the ring and the cinch jerked tight.

Twenty years, twenty-one strokes. I say the necessary short phrases, and then Tess peels down the white underwear, exposing the slim, male hindquarters. They are pale and pink, like a little boy's. But not for long. I take aim, pause, and whip the cane straight into Ground Zero. Thwup.

Liz blinks, the boy says: "Oooh!", and Tess says "One!"[3]

Every now and again, however, one may expect some form of protest:

THE OLD GRANDFATHER clock struck eleven as Harriet finished setting the tasks for the afternoon. She closed her book and rose. Richard followed suit: trembling in every limb, he was devouring his governess with an anxious and supplicating gaze.

She went to the door, drew the bolt, gave a turn of the key in the lock, and then calmly turned the sleeve of her right arm and folded it above the elbow. Richard followed these preparations like one spellbound, as if barely able to conceive the reality they betokened. The young woman looked at him with a faint smile.

"Now, Richard, you will take down your trousers and kneel on that armchair again."

"Oh Miss," he panted,, clasping his hands in entreaty, "please—please, I—I couldn't! Please, Miss—don't beat me!"

She looked at him for a moment with absolute impassivity, her eyes glowing. "I must, Richard," she said. "It is for your own good." For the first time she seemed moved, her voice shaking slightly. "You must be punished. I have decided upon it. And do not expect ever to soften or divert me, Richard," she said, her tone becoming suddenly harsh. "You do not know me yet, I'm afraid! I am very strict, and I do not change my mind. And you, you need a firm hand over you, as your father said—do you remember, Richard? Well, my hand will be firm, you need have no doubt of that. Come, now."

She carried rather than led him to the black leather chair. In her hands, he felt his strength desert him entirely; he let her do as she wished with him, weeping with great infantine sobs, repeating through his tears almost mechanically, "Please, Miss! Oh please, please no!"

Once he was on his knees she did not wait for him to prepare himself; she herself drew his trousers down to his ankles. Richard felt as if he were about to faint. "You will be better without your jacket, too," she said calmly. "We are quite alone, there is no one to disturb us." She unbuttoned his jacket and waistcoat, and pulled them off; then with a swift and expert movement she drew down his short drawers.

But Richard, feeling the chastisement drawing ever nearer, began to

writhe; he tried to retain his drawers as Harriet drew them towards his ankles.

She paused. "Richard," she said coldly, "you are being a very foolish boy. Do you really believe such stupid resistance will do you any good? I have told you, once before, that your punishments will be carried out in a seemly manner—Now, sir, will you cease that struggling, or must I fasten you down?"

"Oh, no, Miss! Don't do that! I'll be quiet..."

"Very well. I advise you to do so." She lifted his shirt and drew it up around his shoulders, then stepping back, she contemplated him for an instant. "Do not think for a moment that I enjoy having to do this, Richard. I am simply acting in your best interests, and I have seen that there is only one course to be taken."[4]

The implicit messages in a command of this type are mixed. On the one hand, it signals as clearly as can be that the culprit is about to undergo the infantile experience of corporal punishment administered to his bare bottom.

On the other hand, there is a further assumption that the culprit will be self-controlled and submissive enough—we might also say brave enough—to cooperate in his own excoriation, simultaneously sanctifying and deriving the maximum spiritual benefit from it. Of course he may be too intimidated to think of doing otherwise, in which case this order both given and obeyed is a satisfactory exercise of authority in its own right. Provided the command *is* obeyed, the hierarchy is reinforced by it and all will be well.

As we have already seen, there may be moments of hesitation or dithering—if not downright mutiny—for which any number of specious excuses may be advanced. These must be overcome by whatever means come easiest: simple willpower is to be preferred, but a threat of force is also perfectly acceptable:

"Just as you wish, ma'am", says the maid; and leaves the room.
A silence falls; there are no more distracting sounds
His Aunt then speaks, in words of measured doom:
"Go to the chair, young man, and take your trousers down!"
He shuffles to the spot ordained in cold dismay
And starts upon the designated task
His frozen fingers cannot find the way
He finds his Aunt's command too much to ask.

"O Auntie, please do let me keep them up!
I'm thirteen now — too old to take them down!
It's not right — " then he wavers at the cusp
On taking note of Auntie's deepening frown.
"Do as I bid! Unbutton right away!
Perhaps you need assistance from a maid?
Your best course is to do just what I say,
Before I summon Ellen to my aid."

"O Aunt, please no! I'm doing it—see here!"
The pallid fingers work with frantic speed
Two buttons at the front, and four at rear,
The neat white trousers slither to the knees.
With breeches gone, all manly spirits fail
He bends as she has bid in trembling fear
Presenting, in the act, a white shirt tail
A paltry veil to mask his quivering rear.

He hears the click of heels as she draws near;
The soft scrape as she takes her sword in hand
He thinks now of the sin that brought him here
And tries to guess what quantity of strokes he'll stand.

In thirteen years he's never been chastised,
No nurse has punished him with stinging slaps,
No slipper ever used to catechise,
The cane was always used on other chaps.

And now, to bend like this, half stripped!
With shirt-tail flapping, right across a chair!
At last, it seems, he's going to be whipped
At least there's one small mercy: he's not bare.
His thigh is touched; he starts; it is her dress,
His shirt-tail's lifted, turn'd up, outside in
And even as he wails a last protest,
His pants have joined his trousers round his shins.

He makes to stand, and tries to pull them up once more
(On nudity, he has not guessed aright),
"Stop struggling, or I'll add six to your score.
While Ellen holds you down—a shameful sight."
He ceases then, in fear of greater rage;
And bends again, face down, with beating heart
Her work's complete; the curtain's up; the stage
Is empty, waiting for the play to start.[5]

The next example is one of reluctance taken to an extreme, and again force has to be threatened before the dreaded command is reluctantly obeyed.

HE WROTE A very good hand—which I do not—and one morning I wanted a manuscript copied; so I gave it to him, telling him to make a fair copy of it as soon as possible, as I wished to post it in the afternoon. It was not a long job, so I told him to have it done in an hour.

At the end of that time I went to the library expecting to find him there with the copy ready for me, but he was not in the room, nor had he even begun the work, for I saw the manuscript lying on the table beside a blank sheet of foolscap paper. I felt very angry, and resolved to birch him as soon as he made his appearance. I had not got a rod, but there were several birch trees growing in the grounds, so I went out and cut a few long, slender, sappy, green twigs, and soon made a first-rate rod; and, as I swished it in the air to test its flexibility, I said to myself: "Ah! master Francis, this will make your bottom smart." I went back to the library, put the rod in a drawer...

In about an hour's time Frank came into the room. I put down the book and rose from my seat. "Why have you not copied the manuscript?" I said sternly, looking him full in the face, as he stood before me.

"Oh, I couldn't be bothered," he replied flippantly. I was very much astonished, as he had never answered me in such a saucy way before.

"You have deliberately disobeyed me, and you have answered me improperly. I am going to birch you," I said, angrily taking the rod out of the drawer, and holding it up for him to see. He was quite taken aback at the sight of it, and very much frightened; his face became scarlet. and he began to tremble.

"Oh! don't birch me! Please don't birch me!" he exclaimed, bursting into tears, and stretching out his hands towards me, with an imploring gesture.

"Let down your trousers, and lie across the end of the sofa!" said I, sharply.

"Oh! Oh! Oh!" he cried. "I know I deserve to be punished, but please don't birch me. Punish me in any other way but that."

"I will not punish you in any other way. Let down your trousers at once. I did not think you were a coward."

"I am not a coward. I am not afraid of the pain. I can bear it. But I am ashamed to let down my trousers before you," he sobbed out.

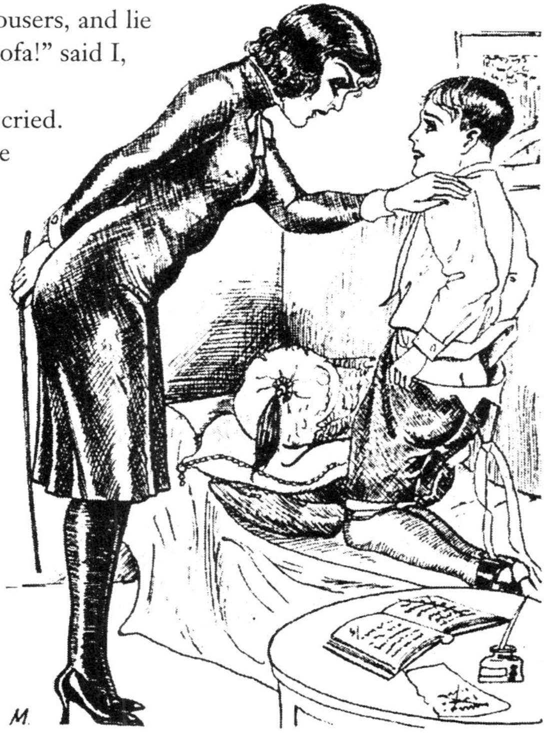

"Don't be silly!... Now unbutton! Look sharp!"

"Oh! don't make me let down my trousers," he again said, beseechingly. I lost patience. "If you don't at once obey me, I will send for Wilson and get him to take down your trousers, and then hold you on his back while I flog you," I said, in a loud voice.

"Oh! don't do that. Don't do that!" he cried out, in terrified accents, with a look of horror on his face. "I will let down my trousers."

He tumed half aside, and with trembling fingers, unfastened his braces, and unbuttoned his trousers, letting them slip down to his knees; and then he laid himself across the end of the sofa, with his hands resting on the floor at one side, and the tips of his toes on the other side, thus bringing his body into a curve with his bottom well raised up—in a splendid position for receiving the rod. I could not understand why he had made so much fuss about letting down his trousers.[6]

It is difficult not to feel a little sympathy for those who experience real anguish on receipt of this shaming command for the very first time in their lives, and as experts know, it greatly helps all concerned if the event is set into a formal framework with a precise structure of sequential commands, especially when these add grace to the proceedings and are as far removed from institutional "barking" as one can imagine:

WHEN I TELL a guilty boy to prepare himself for punishment I do so in a reasonable voice, and in a calm manner, thus:–

Now, [Surname], *you know why you are here. Go directly and stand by that chair by the wall.*

And when he has done so:–

Unfasten your trousers and let them down

And when he has done so:–

Bend over the chair and hold the legs in front, with your face as close as

> *possible to the seat. Keep your feet and knees together and your legs perfectly straight.*

And when he has done so:–

> *I am now going to give you six strokes of the cane* [or whatever punishment you have decreed]. *If you keep quite still and remain as quiet as you can it will soon be over. If you move, or attempt to get up, or speak without permission, I shall take down your drawers before continuing with the punishment. If you move or speak a second time we shall start again at the beginning. Do you understand?*

Assuming all has gone as it is here set out, I then take the rod and administer the punishment. However, some boys—especially those being punished this way for the first time—are ashamed to take their trousers down before a female; on these occasions a different approach is necessary.

The most important thing I wish to say is that I still do not raise my voice—it is quite possible to bend a potential mutineer to your dominion without shouting. Here is a boy afraid to take his trousers down; he is afraid to refuse also, but at the moment he is more afraid to strip.

> [Surname], *I warn you to do as I bid. Take down your trousers and bend over.*

And when he still refuses:–

> [Surname], *this is your last chance. In a moment I am going to give the order one last time. If you refuse again I shall take your trousers down myself. Then I shall tie you across that chair. Then I shall cane you until you can't sit down for a week, and you will spend that week dressed in girl's clothes wearing a placard saying* COWARD. *I hope you understand. Now, for the last time: do as I have ordered.*

If he still refuses then of course you must carry out your threat.[7]

A compressed version of the same exchange—in poetical form, and from the opposite viewpoint—may be found in *Sweet Retribution:*

There's a moment of cold silence, and I wait to hear the Word.
She speaks—and straight away I know my prayer has not been heard.
"For hooligan behaviour," says Miss Linnet, with a frown,
"I shall cane you. Stand beside the chair and take your trousers down."
Time stops; my fingers fumble; then Miss Linnet says: "Make haste!
If I have to come and help you it'll add to your disgrace."
The buttons give—the trousers slide—they hover in mid-air.
They fall. Miss Linnet orders me to bend across the chair.[8]

WHEN DEALING WITH females, the appropriate commands are of course different, though precisely equivalent, with (girls being girls) outright resistance or overmuch hesitation even more at a discount:

"NOW, DORA, you know that your mother has requested me to whip you soundly. And I warn you that if you are not perfectly submissive, I will double your punishment. Take off your frocks, stays and drawers; fold them up tidily, and put them on the sofa."

The tears welled up in the girl's eyes, and began to trickle down her cheeks; and she hesitated for a moment; then she took off her smart little satin corset. Then, putting her hands under her petticoats, she slowly unfastened her drawers, let them slip down her legs to the floor, and stepped clear of the dainty, lace-trimmed garment. Then, with trembling fingers, she folded up the articles, placed them on the sofa, and stood, with downcast, tearful eyes, waiting for further orders.

"Now, get the rod; hand it to me, with a curtsey; say that you have misbehaved; and ask me if I will be pleased to give you a good whipping."

Dora's pale face flushed when she heard the humiliating order, and the tears ran quicker down her cheeks, but she did not move.

"Obey me at once. Every time I have to repeat an order, I will add to your punishment," said the governess, stamping her foot.

The girl was cowed. She got the rod, and handed it to the governess, with a curtsey, saying in a low, trembling voice: "I have been naughty. Please give me a good whipping."

"I will," said the governess.[9]

The second also contains a hint of rebellion—instantly quashed:

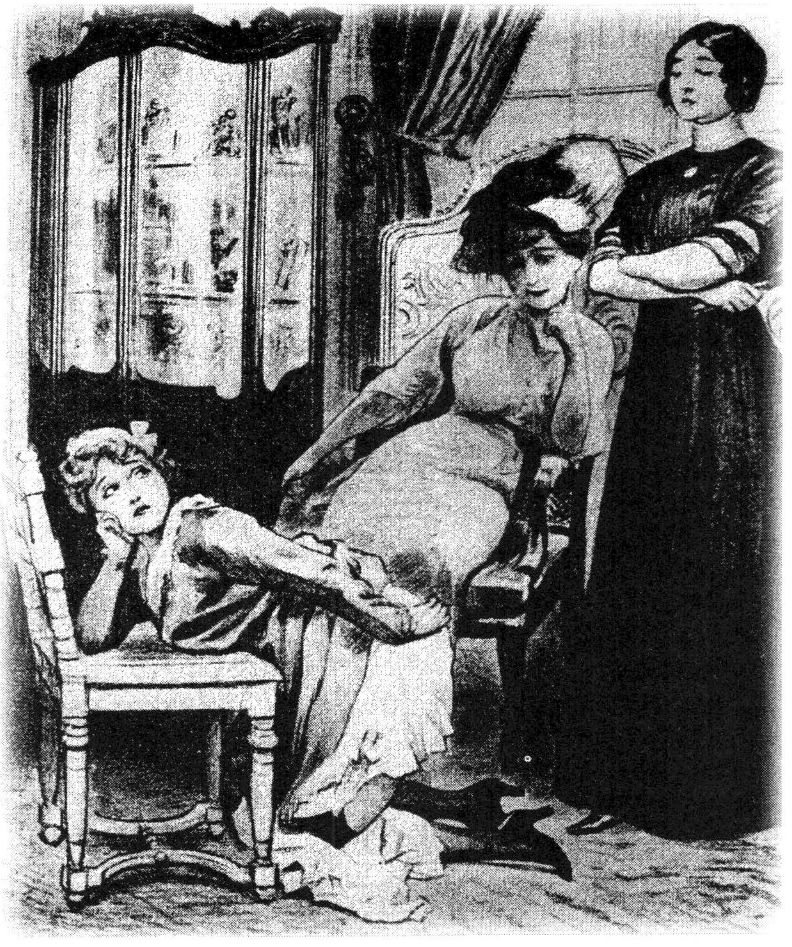

"Oh Mama, don't smack me! Oh Mama, please—no!
If you do that Hermione and Daphne will know!"
As she utters these words in a whine of dismay
They both hear some noises, not far away,
Which indicate that, in the next room but one,
A separate chastisement's already begun
"Take off your frock, girl—don't stand there and moan!
Hermione and Daphne have woes of their own.

Do as I bid, Lucy. Take off your dress.
And do it this instant, young lady, unless
You want me to do it. For if I have to
I'll take off your frock and your petticoats too
Then I'll march you in where the others can see
Your disgrace as I put you over my knee.
I'll take down your knickers in front of them all.
And afterwards you can stand in the hall
For a good half an hour with your hands on your head
For once you'll be grateful to be sent to bed!"
Lucy gropes for the hooks, her eyes running water
The image of everyone's penitent daughter
The frock starts to slide; it slithers; it lands
At her feet. "Hang it up!" her mother commands.
"Now—off with those petticoats! Hang those up too.
Your clothes cost good money. It's about time that you
Paid much more attention to things of that kind.
Now—undo the strings of your drawers behind!"
At this last fierce instruction poor Lucy breaks down.
Heedless of her Mama's gathering frown.
A hand reaches out, and her daughter is seized.
Hauled forward to topple across Mama's knees.
While one mighty elbow restrains her in place
Mother's right hand starts to fumble with lace.
The strings are untied; the knickers descend
Revealed is poor Lucy's defenceless rear end...[10]

For a style of compliance that is the very epitome of meek submission, the following passage is hard to match—dominance is total and obedience instant.

BETTY... HAD expected the conversation would take this turn, yet had foolishly hoped she might be mistaken. This was, in a sense, worse than a whipping but what could she do? When her mother called her Baby it always had a hypnotic effect upon her. Fifteen already, and as big as the average girl of eighteen, and lovely to look at, she should have felt humiliated at being regarded as a baby, and to be called that even before strangers. Instead, the effect on her was a strangely opposite one, for it stirred a desire to nestle up close and put her head on her mother's breast, to close her eyes and be held tight and fondled. Obediently she began: "When mother is displeased with me, Uncle Arthur…" she paused.

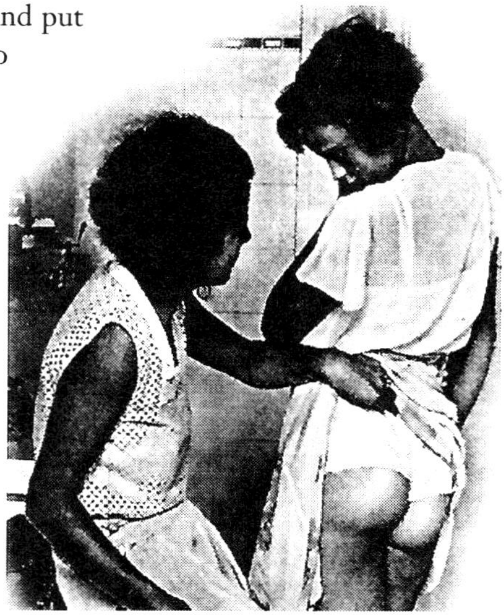

"Yes dear, go right ahead, I am listening," he said softly, trying to control his voice.

"She sends me to my room where I have to make myself ready for punishment and wait for her. I take off everything except my knickers or girdle, then I get the instrument she wishes to use, as well as wrist and ankle belts, from the drawer, put them on the table next to the bed, and lie down. After mother enters I have to assume whatever position she demands, kiss the instrument, and hand it over. Then mother whips me."

"You forgot something, dear," cautioned her mother, gently.

"What, mother?" The child looked puzzled.

"What do I do with your knickers or girdle?"

"Oh, you pull them down and I have to help you with my legs to get them off."

"That's right. Go on."

"Then you whip me." She paused. "After that…,"

"No, no, no!" Eleanor raised her voice. "Not so fast! Where do I whip you? On what part of your body?"

Betty swallowed hard.

"You whip me on my… on my bottom. Then…"

"Wait just a minute!" She pulled her back on her lap still closer to her breast. "You don't have to tell this to me, dear. Address yourself to Uncle Arthur, please. Now go back to where you were before these interruptions. Tell Uncle Arthur what I do with your panties."

"Mother pulls my panties or girdle off, Uncle Arthur, and I help her with my legs," she resumed, obediently, like a perfectly trained pony to the bridle of its master. "Then she whips me… on my… bare bottom"—the telling seemed easier after the obstacle of those words— "with the strap or martinet, or sometimes the back of my hairbrush or a ruler, until she thinks I've had enough. Then mother sits me on her lap and asks me questions about the thing I displeased her about."

"'About the thing I displeased her about'! Such English dear!" interrupted her mother, reprovingly.

"Excuse me, mother, I mean the thing you were displeased about, and whether I deserve to be punished for it." Remembering to address Uncle Arthur, she continued. "At the end I have to say, 'Yes, mother, I deserved to be punished for that. Thank you for whipping me.' Then I kiss the strap again and kiss mother, and it's all over."[11]

SO FAR IN this chapter we have dealt with what may be termed the direct type of command—that is, one given at (or slightly before) the moment of actual punishment. There is no particular reason why this should be so, nor indeed why the two distinct stages of self-unbreeching (apart from any ancillary stages that might occur to you) should not be relatively widely separated in time, in order to extract the maximum psychological advantage from each. Nor, if we are to be truly flexible, is there any reason why the first stage of *déculottage* should not be carried out by the culprit even before he comes into your presence. He will have to be informed of your will in this regard beforehand, of course, but there are many creative ways of so doing (a note delivered by hand of a maidservant is an excellent way); or one might with ease establish a Rule about such matters. To be obliged to appear in the presence of his punisher already *bien déculotté*—which might of course mean passing through a busy household beforehand in that same dismal condition—introduces an extra portion of shame at no extra effort to oneself.

I WAS IN a children's home from just before the war ended until about 1951. It was a grim place with a lot of smacking, mostly from the Matron, a Mrs Tilley who I remember as a great fat woman who never smiled—she was terrifying. When I'd been there about a month two boys, older than me, decided to run away. They made their plans but somehow they were found out and all was revealed to Ma Tilley. She said: "Tell them to come and see me before they set out, won't you?"

The upshot was that we were all assembled in the hall, and these two were brought in, wearing just underpants and vests. The first boy was told to pull down his pants and bend over the desk. He refused. They grabbed him and bent him over—down came his pants, and he was slippered by Ma Tilley for what seemed like a week. His backside was as red as fire but I'll always remember that he never cried. The second boy pulled his pants down when she told him, but it didn't do him much good. He got just as many and cried a lot more.[12]

Here is the same general sort of idea, in a still more baroque—albeit fictional—form.

EARLIER THAT morning William had been woken from a strange and fitful sleep by the sound of chairs scraping and girls' voices whispering and

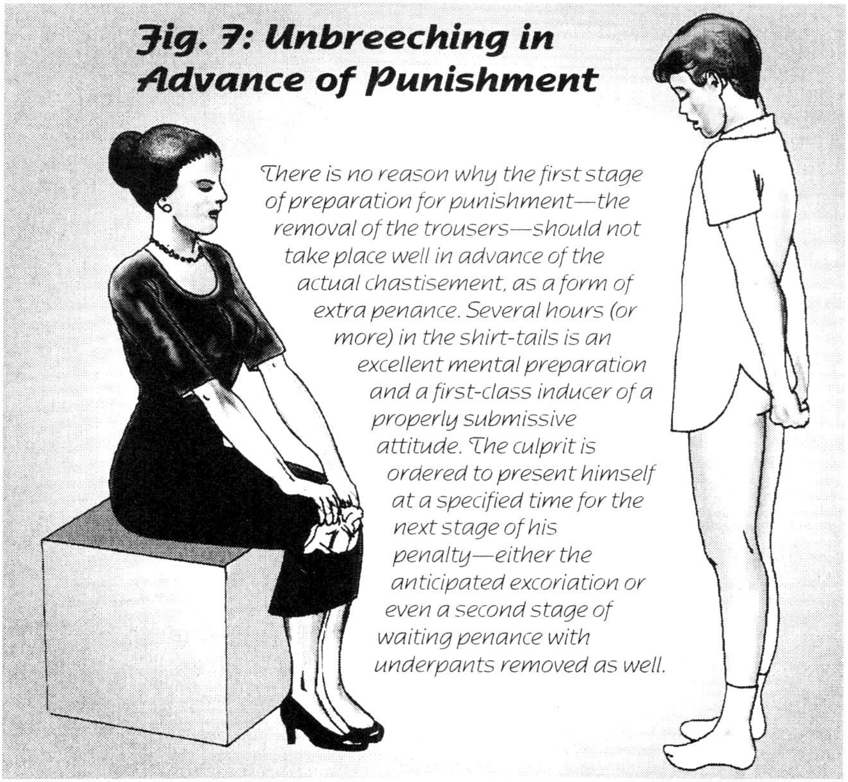

Fig. 7: Unbreeching in Advance of Punishment

giggling. At first he thought he was still dreaming. Something felt rather strange—it was as if he had been put over his aunt's knee for a spanking, only it wasn't her knee—it was bigger, wider and flatter; like a kind of soft and padded desk. And the voices—he remembered Lucy and her friends in the drawing-room on that day that the incident had happened. But this time he wasn't being beaten: this time he was just relaxing, dozing. But where was he? Perhaps he was in a field—he could feel cool air on his bottom and the backs of his legs. It actually felt rather pleasant and comfortable, in an odd sort of way.

Suddenly he remembered, and woke with a start. He was bent, face-down, across the end of his bed and his pyjama trousers were down around his ankles. The other eleven boys were similarly arranged. He looked towards the door and saw some third-form girls arranging two chairs at the top end of the dorm. They saw his head turn, giggled, and ran from the room, slamming the door behind them.

"Overs", he remembered. Matron had made them all bend over their beds last night, and had pulled down each boy's trousers in turn. She had instructed them, on the direst pains, to stay like that until they were told to get up, some time the following morning. But what was the meaning of the chairs? And when would they be allowed to stand up and get dressed? Breakfast time came and went. He heard the other children laughing and chattering in the corridors. What a strange punishment this was![13]

A relatively similar, though tactically different, effect may be achieved by introducing a unconventional pause into an otherwise standard unbreeching ceremony.

FOR VERY SERIOUS offences there would be what were known to us as 'public spankations'. Of these, there were only two during the four years I was at the school. The first took place after a weak assistant master had entirely failed to control a prep. which gradually dissolved into a general, anarchic rag. Everyone was wondering why the master was apparently doing nothing. In fact, he was taking names to report to Mr Stow. After evening prayers that night three of the principal offenders, picked at random, were told to come up to the front and take down their trousers. They were then beaten hard with the fives bat, before the eyes of the whole school.

> The second occasion was when three quite senior boys, members of one of the classes who were supposed to do their prep. uninvigilated in their classroom, climbed out of the window and went for a night walk on the near-by common. As ill luck would have it, they ran into the Headmaster's brother, Sir Alexander Stow, who happened to be taking a walk. Naturally, he reported them. They, too, were publicly spanked—five each with the fives bat.
>
> One thing about this I have never forgotten. Mr Morris's place at prayers was at the back of the big schoolroom where we assembled. During the pause while the culprits were taking down their trousers and Mr Stow had gone out of the room to get the fives bat, the silence was broken by the sound of Mr Morris shambling up the length of the room. He drew out a bench and placed it exactly at a right angle to the desk over which the three boys would have to bend. On this he sat down, leaning forward with his elbows on his knees and his hands together, with the air of a connoisseur who was not going to miss anything.[14]

Keeping a culprit waiting in fear and trembling with his trousers around his ankles while you go in search of the instrument of chastisement (as above) is but one form of this gambit. There is also the exact reverse—sending him to an appointed place to assume this condition and await your arrival. He may at your pleasure be dispatched trouserless (or hobbled by downfallen trousers) to fetch the rod for himself, or even—if you are fortunate enough to live in a secluded and well-wooded place—to manufacture it for himself from birch, willow or hazel. In fact, virtually any disciplinary "fatigue" task may be performed in a trouserless or even bare-bottomed condition for extra piquancy, either as a discipline in its own right, or, as here, when it is an understood thing that when this sanction is eventually lifted, it will only be because a thrashing—no less painful because postponed—has just been administered. Properly managed, such procedures can closely resemble electrical storms—a period of growing tension followed by a few minutes of sound and fury and finally a healthy, life-giving shower of rain!

I may be a traditionalist, but I do feel that the return of breeches after such a prolonged separation ought to be signified with some form of minor ceremony—after all, it is the real moment of forgiveness: as well as being a curious echo of the custom of "breeching" little boys in order to signify the end of babyhood. Personally I am in favour of the mistress herself re-instating the garments, up to the last brace-button: not only is this a tender, maternal and thoroughly charming act, it also reinforces the concept that *his* breeches are *your* domain, to do with as you will. That he wears them at all is by your Grace and Favour alone.

CHAPTER NOTES

1. "Betsy Fry" from *Venus School-mistress, Ashbee (London), 185?.*
2. *The Romance of Lust*
3. *SR.*
4. *Harriet Marwood, Governess* by Miles Underwood, 1967, various editions.
5. "An Aunt Does Her Duty" *(Guide).*
6. *Frank & I*
7. *Guide.*
8. *SR.*
9. *Frank & I.*
10. "The Nursery Tea" (*QoG*).
11. *Happy Tears* by Norman Grace.
12. Letter to the Alice Kerr-Sutherland Society, 1994.
13. *Linton Abbey*
14. *The Day Gone By* (Richard Adams)

4: The Communiqué of Shame

"Unbutton! Let down!" These words, with a frown,
Do a great deal to quicken my fear
In a frenzy of speed I haul trousers to knees
And an icy voice orders "come here!"[1]

WHEN I was a lot younger than I am today, I once visited the house of a school friend (female). The family left the district soon afterwards and this was the only time I visited her. This girl had a brother, as many did; and the brother was less well-behaved than my friend, as so many are. At tea, taken with my friend's friendly, dark-haired mother, he showed off a great deal (as so many do), until the mother, without sounding the slightest bit angry, said: "Donald, start behaving properly if you want to keep your trousers on." It was said with perfect calm, and I have never forgotten the instant effect upon the brother; as deep a blush as I have ever seen in my life. He was utterly shocked and quelled by these words, in a way that the more commonly-encountered (in those days) threat to smack would not have achieved. His mother did not threaten to smack him if he continued to misbehave—or if she did, it was in an oblique fashion. Instead she promised to remove his trousers… Whether or not a smacking would be the inevitable sequel of such a manœuvre, or whether the confiscation alone would be con-

sidered punishment enough, I never discovered.

Since that time I have often overheard irate mothers threatening, not necessarily to smack their naughty sons, but to take their trousers down—smacking is also clearly implied, but the threat to remove trousers is clearly the more potent of the two. It surely follows that these erstwhile disciplinarian mothers have in the past discovered, empirically no doubt, that the specific threat to unbreech—often without any mention of spanking—is more than often enough to evoke the required obedience. If true, this is an interesting corroboration of my own theory that unbreeching is actually a more traumatic procedure than smacking. It is also proof that the shaming words have a power of their own.

I WAS NEARLY seventeen. One afternoon, at the end of a short holiday I had taken in Naples with my parents, walking by myself down a crowded street, I saw a big, handsome woman, the proprietor of a trattoria, standing in the doorway of her restaurant and watching a boy of about thirteen years, a good-looking brown-haired boy, with well-shaped limbs and body, who was displaying a disrespectful, sulky demeanour towards his mother and answering her in the same spirit. This woman thereupon loudly urged the latter to punish him as he deserved, and in terms that I can never forget:

"Why don't you give him a spanking? If he were up to me, he would already have his trousers down, and I tell you it would be a good one! There's nothing else these young gentlemen fear more than spankings! Good ones, in front of everybody else! With their trousers well down so that their bottoms are on view!"

I was utterly transfixed by hearing these crude words spoken aloud with such expressive and extraordinary energy. The boy was already big and robust for his age, to judge by the well-made legs that were revealed under his short trousers. He had a prominent bottom. Perhaps it had been this particularity (noticed also by myself) which had suggested to the vigorous woman the idea of such a correction, which she—35 years or so, tall and powerful, with strong arms—was plainly capable of inflicting without undue effort. She was obviously able to do the same to an even bigger and older boy and the idea came to me in a flash that I myself, aged sixteen and a half, would find it impossible to escape if it should please her to deal with me in this way. She would without difficulty unbreech me by sheer force, against all my resistance...

These ideas came at once, with clarity and rapidity, to engrave themselves on my soul, like the phrase 'trousers down' which I had heard for the first time uttered by a woman... Yes, engraved—like the memory of her hand that, in gestures full of meaning accompanied and enhanced each of her words, waved about in an explicit way, stretched flat as if already in action, testifying to the supreme quality of the spanking she was all too ready to inflict.[2]

Another story in the same book offers a good example of the deadly words being used *after* a chastisement, specifically in order to intimidate the witnesses. A new and formidable schoolmistress has just administered a resounding—and wholly unexpected—bare-bottom spanking to the biggest boy in the class:

"YOU HAVE SEEN, my little friends, how your comrade has been well spanked. This will be repeated each time one of you misbehaves. I have

studied you all over the last two days and I know who are good, and who are naughty. On your side, you have seen me at work—with the biggest of you! So you know what I'm capable of. Make sure this knowledge is to your profit. Remember I'm strong enough to spank you—and not on the seats of your trousers, either, but with them taken down, as you have just seen."[3]

Words, phrases and litanies have an enormous part to play in discipline. Here is an example of the device being used in a general disciplinary sense: it is not specifically related to unbreeching, but is nevertheless worth including, if only because of the artful way it involves the culprit in the dialogue:

> IT WAS A Sunday morning. Mlle. Fosse would go to Moorfields to her father confessor, and attend an afternoon lecture; so as soon as I had done luncheon I told Jane and the other two servants they might go out for the afternoon, and return by half-past six or seven, as I would dispense with dinner if Margaret the cook would have something nice for supper, and Charlie could answer my bell if anything was wanted.
>
> As soon as the house was clear, and I knew the cook liked the society of her pots and pans too much to think of leaving the precincts of the

kitchen, I rang for my page, and ordered him to bring a lemon, some iced water, sugar, &c., and seeing that he had dressed himself with scrupulous care in case I summoned him, I said, "Charlie, I'm glad to see you are particular about your appearance, although there is no one at home."

CHARLIE, with great modesty — "But you, Miss, are my mistress, and I always wish to show you the greatest possible respect even when you are not quite alone."

ROSA — "Indeed, sir, you profess great respect for me, and seem afraid hardly to lift your eyes, as if I was too awful to look at, but I have my doubts about your goodness; will you please fetch me a rather long packet you will find wrapped in paper on the library table."

He soon returned with the parcel, and I proceeded to open it as he stood before me, awaiting his dismissal or further orders. The paper was removed, and I flourished before his face (which rather flushed at the sight) a good long rod of fresh green birch, tied up with scarlet ribbons. "Do you know what this is for, sir?" I asked the astonished boy.

CHARLIE, in some little confusion—"Ah! Oh! I don't know—unless it's what's used for whipping young ladies at school."

ROSA—"And why not boys, you stupid?"

CHARLIE—"Ah! Miss Rosa, you're making fun of me, they use canes and straps to boys—but—but—"

ROSA—"Out with what you are going to say, I'm the only one that can hear it."

CHARLIE—"Why—why—(turning quite scarlet), the thought came into my head that you might be going to whip me."[4]

For an excellent example of purely rhetorical deployment, let us return to the story of Gabriel and his cousin, the narrator, unbreeched and spanked *à deux* by the tennis teacher (Mlle. Hermance), and now about to suffer a reprise punishment, this time in the presence of other females:

SHE STRETCHED HIM across her lap exactly like the day before. The three sisters remained in their place following with their eyes, and with the interest she compelled, the lesson in unbreeching which they were now given by their mistress.

It was Madame Pujol who broke the silence.

> "See, girls, how a boy's trousers are taken down. This will help you, on the occasions when you have to deal with a son and no other method will serve. All of them deserve spanking from time to time. But don't forget that, for boys, the most humiliating aspect, as Hermance will demonstrate in a moment, is to have their trousers taken down in front of witnesses. How Gabriel has gone red! And the other who awaits his turn! See the look on his face, knowing that he also is going to be unbreeched in front of us... Unbreeched by a young woman in front of another woman and three young ladies! Is that shameful enough for a boy?[5]

Here are three more examples of the same device being used to deadly effect. In two of them the shaming commentary depends for fullest effect upon the invocation of witnesses—both real and imaginary.

> "COME HERE at once, James," she summoned the boy.
>
> The unlucky boy caught his breath.
>
> "Miss", he began to whimper, "Forgive me!... not... in front of... Bridget."
>
> "Don't argue! Come here!" commanded the Governess.
>
> James tried to flee, but his legs refused to obey. Meanwhile Barbara fixed him with her eye—he *had* to obey. Trembling, he stumbled over to her and she seized him by his hands.
>
> "I shall not give you your full punishment immediately," shebegan, "I want merely first of all to show Bridget how one handles naughty boys, no matter what age they are."
>
> She spread her legs apart and clamped James between her knees, turned him round, bent him over her left thigh, and held him firmly around the waist with her left arm. James found himself in the classic position of boys about to receive the rod.
>
> He made no resistance, for he knew that it was perfectly hopeless and would only make his position worse.
>
> But the humiliation was dreadful to him. To receive the rod at all, let alone undergo it in the presence of the housemaid!
>
> He thought he would die when he felt Barbara's fingers unbuttoning his trousers and underpants and taking them down to his knees, and could not suppress a despairing squeal as the governess pulled up his shirt.

"You see, Bridget, it isn't difficult to take a big boy's trousers down," instructed Barbara. "Do you not think that he would rather sink into the earth for very shame? Oh, James, shame on you! Think—to be prepared for the rod, to have to display your bare bottom in front of two women and then to be beaten on it with my hand! Will you steal chocolate again? Answer me! Will you?"

"Oh no, no, Miss! I'll never do it again!" whimpered the boy in his excruciating position.

"And you shall receive the rod, and really be punished for your fault. You will get a respectable number of strokes, but only a sample of what awaits you tonight. Then at bedtime you will receive your full punishment. With birch and strap!"

While Barbara has been speaking to the boy in this fashion, she still had not begun to beat him. She now commenced to draw his underpants a little further down, and his shirt a little further up; she pressed his legs a little tighter between her own, and her hand, lying on his bottom, moved softly up and down. For him the contrast between the coolness of the air and the warmth of her hand brought home to him the shame of his nudity.[6]

IN THE BEGINNING both my sister and I found it puzzling when the stepmother mysteriously came into the room or even merely stuck her head in the door, motioned with her forefinger and called out, "Edith, come over here!" Little by little, however, we understood what it signified: the birch rod, the rear flap of the drawers pulled down in order to lay bare the bottom, always face downward, across her lap or—especially as we grew older—across a chair! And while she once more rebuked the culprit for her misbehaviour, she bared the bottom with great care while deploring the necessity to birch such a big girl on her bare—yes, on her bare—bottom. She would lay such a special emphasis on "bare" that one simply felt like crawling into the earth for shame.[7]

WHAT I LIKE, above all, is to correct him on returning from evenings out where he has been particularly brilliant. On that subject, I'm going to recount to you his latest... It is still totally fresh in my memory (if not his bottom) for it dates as recently as yesterday evening.

Thus, yesterday, with regard to one of his recent successes, he was invited, me too, to a banquet at which he was the chairman. The guests of both sexes were many but carefully chosen, extremely well-dressed. During dessert, there were, of course, speeches. My husband concluded the series and had a big success, because he gave a very spirited performance. After the banquet, everybody came to congratulate him, and you can imagine how happy and proud we were, my dear husband and I.

After, we returned home alone in the car, talking about the evening and the triumph that my husband had achieved. When we were in our bedroom, he repeated one more time with a naive pride: "Told you so. What a success!"

I interrupted and said: "It seems to me that you are quite arrogant, my friend. It is time that I bring a little humility to you. You are going to give me the pleasure of preparing yourself to receive a spanking."

"Oh… "

"And right away, you hear?"

He had nothing else to say. He undressed, keeping on only his shirt and underpants, both in silk, and his socks and shoes. I like to see him in that way, just his pants and socks. He has the look of a big kid. For my part, I remained dressed in my low-cut evening dress, with its bare back and no sleeves.

"Kneel on this armchair," I told him.

He obeyed me and knelt, leaning forward with his arms on the back of the armchair.

"Raise your bottom. Better than that!"

He raised it properly.

"Now, remove them yourself."

He unbuttoned his pants and pulled them down to his knees.

"Good. Now lift your shirt."

He raised it high, revealing his bare bottom.

"Further... And at the front too."

He did as he was ordered.

Then I approached him and placed my left arm around him. His buttocks were presented clearly before me. I examined them with my right hand before saying to him:

"Tell me, have you no shame! Have you no real shame? What shame I would have in your place. Barely half an hour ago, Monsieur was strutting about, putting on airs and graces among the ladies and gentlemen, addressing them with beautiful compliments, smiling at his own triumphs! And now, thirty minutes later, here he is on his knees, my arm holding him around the waist, trouserless, his shirt tucked up back and front, holding out his bare bottom, and waiting to receive a good spanking like an unbearable brat awaiting his punishment. Monsieur is no longer proud! He no longer says: what success! What he is going to say soon is: what a spanking! Go on, Monsieur, show me this behind, hold it high, that I can spank it!"

I whacked him furiously. I swear he received, yesterday evening, one of the best spankings that he had had in his life! When I was exhausted, I took him by the ear and led him into the corner. I tucked his shirt up above his back so that it would stay up by itself. Also I had crossed his arms, and I calmly sat in the armchair after I had spanked him.

It was amusing to see him like that, his arms crossed, his shirt tucked up, his pants around his ankles, with his black socks, his calves and naked thighs, and especially, in the middle, the beautiful middle, his completely red bottom still trembling from the severe correction I had given it.

"If Madame X," I said to him, "saw you now, spanked brat in the corner, she would laugh, she who always looks at you so lovingly. And Madame Y who admires you so much, would she believe her eyes? And Madame Z who asked you for your autograph, she would be ashamed of you if she found you with your red bottom!"

And I went through a list of names of the ladies, one after another.[8]

1. "Miss Hathaway" (*QoG)*
2. *Les Mains Chéries*
3. Ibid.
4. *The Pearl,* Volume II.
5. *Les Mains Chéries*
6. From a German translation of a (Fr.) novel by "Aimé van Rod" (c.1925). Curiously, a scene very similar in content appears in an early draft of the novel eventually published as *Harriet Marwood, Governess.*
7. *Confessions & Experiences.*
8. Letter published as appendix in *Memoires d'un Dominatrice* (Liane Laure), Paris, c. 1934.

5: The Accoutrements of Discipline

The removal of Edward's trousers was a double pleasure; for underneath the velvet shorts he wore, there was a pair of knickers made of lace which must have cost a fabulous sum...[1]

IT IS PERFECTLY reasonable to assume that, just as the clothes worn by the culprit at the time of his unbreeching can, by their very design, either ease or hinder the task of the *déculotteuse*, so those same clothes may, and for similar reasons, increase or retard her enjoyment of the small duty she has set herself.

It is one thing to tackle everyday, utilitarian buttons, clasps and other fastenings; another to do so with any degree of sensual pleasure outside that furnished by the act itself. If *déculottage* is not a sensual

Fig. 8: Styles of Male Outer Garment

1. Knicker-bockers (knee breeches). 2. Ordinary trousers with belt. 3. Culottes with braces (suspenders). 4. High-waisted Spanish trousers with back buttons. 5. Sailor suit with short trousers (braces worn underneath jacket). 6. Lady's maid in starchy black dress with 1 or more linen petticoats.

experience, I do not know what this book has been about so far; and the plain truth is that, for many *déculotteuses*, sensory pleasure may be greatly enhanced by having to deal with pleasant, tactile materials rather than rough, workaday ones: and if these are in some way "feminine" or sissy, it is once again a reinforcement of the notion that his lower garments are your domain. You undress him as you please, therefore you may dress him as you please. And, in selecting garments which it is an especial pleasure to unfasten and pull down, you may discover that these same garments so often turn out to be "feminine" that you may even, as so many do, formulate this empirical observation into a regular practice, with its own rules and disciplines. And every now and again you will also find that the punishment particularly fits the crime, as the two following poems illustrate:

THE NEXT TIME on my maid, Ladow;
A strong-back'd wench, who takes delight
In horsing naughty boys and girls,
I whipt upon her back last night
A French Duke, and two English Earls:
The first of which, with frock and sash,
I drest just like a full grown Miss;
Then gave him many a vig'rous lash,
For giving footman John a kiss;
I taught this fancied Miss a dance—
I made him caper to the ceiling:
He swore no Ma'emoiselle in France
convinc'd him more that he had feeling![2]

"HOW MANY," Milady now asks, "did you say
Are due to be birched on this Punishment Day?"
"Two culprits, your Ladyship", Matron replies
"For dreadful debauchery, and telling of lies."
"Debauchery, Matron?"—"Milady, 'tis so.
The vile thing occurred not more than two days ago.
When the villains were found, there was naught they could say.
And I vowed they'd be flogged on this Punishment Day!"
"They were found do you say? What condition was this?"
"Milady, I hesitate—" "Yet I insist."

"I'll tell you, Milady, with sadness and grief
For it shows how the Evil One works his mischief.
These two, Edwin Murray and Mortimer Stead
Consorted together; they shared the same bed!"
"And what style of punishment have you decreed,
A fitting riposte to this depravé deed?"
"Milady, to chastise these villainous hides,
Two dozen, I thought, that's a dozen each side."
"And what are the ages?"—"Both have fourteen years."
"Then twenty-four lashes is too much to bear."
"Milady?"—"Dear Matron, our cause in this place,
Is to salvage the debris of our human race
And by all means—that includes Justice's Sword—
To bring all our charges the Love of the Lord.
The Rod is our ally, our servant, our friend
But not, of itself, the only sure end.
To punish too violently is a mistake
The souls in our keeping are not ours to break.
A surfeit of cruelty draws the wrong mood
And two dozen birch-strokes will surely draw blood."
The Matron dissembles; in fact she's astounded
To hear views such as these from Milady propounded.
She's amazed (it wouldn't be too much to say)
To hear such opinions on Punishment Day!
Yet she errs in her judgment: M'Lady's not mild;
Neither sparing the rod, nor spoiling the child
"This crime is so shameful, that Shaming must play
A particular part in this Punishment Day!
A notion I have: it's to take these two flirts
And forcibly dress them in maidchildren's skirts.
With pinafores, bonnets and black stockings too
It ought to provide the most interesting view!
When birching a boy, the mode I prefer
Is the untrussèd youth bending over a chair
Or a stool or a table or any low thing
To accept, on his own, the chastisement's sting.
By displaying the courage a boy should possess
He salvages dignity under duress.

But from girls we expect less heroics, I fear
Less stoic than boys, girls are more prone to tears
They stand up, and shuffle, and cover, and fend
And try to evade the ferrule that descends.
For this reason they're horsed—it prevents further fuss
An ideal posture for being untrussed.
If we treat your two culprits like wise, I should say
Then they'll always remember this Punishment Day!
To be whipp'd like two girls for their degraded deed?
A dozen sharp strokes will be all that we need!"
The Matron's convinced; she summons a nurse
And raps out commands in sentences terse.
The nurse drops a curtsey and hastens away
There now comes a lull in this Punishment Day!
A minute—ten minutes—of silence are shared
Then enters a nurse: "Madam, all is prepared!"
Her Ladyship nods, and then Matron does too
A doleful procession then comes into view
Two great girls, it seems, are led to the dais
Their smocks and their pinafores neatly in place
Their bonnets are fastened, their girdles are clasped
Each carries a birch-spray in trembling grasp.
And, kneeling to offer the soon—to-be-used rods,
Each "maid" humbly begs to be properly flogged.
Like girls they are horsed; and their smocks are pulled high
Exposing white bloomer as far as mid-thigh
These drawers are unfastened and eased off the hips
Each bottom prepared for the kiss of the whip.
And as the birch hovers, dear reader, I pray
Let's take our leave of this Punishment Day![3]

But settings are not always institutional—and public. Even more exciting degradations may be applied in private:

THE FINERY THAT I placed at his disposal was feminine apparel. In order to gather together everything of my choice, I must have walked far, because I held firm, in my choice of underwear, for open knickers. Yet it was that piece of lingerie that caused difficulties, for the totally enclosed knickers had superseded everywhere.

I must have suffered the mocking smiles of a great many of the merchants, but I finally succeeded even though I was pushed almost to the end of my tether.

Those for Jerome to begin with!

He made a painful grimace when I laced the corset onto the short and fine feminine chemise. And his emotion became more marked when I buttoned the lace knickers to his waist. I covered that very quickly with a slip and a small black sleeved dress. Black, likewise, were the new stockings that I had matched with patent shoes. Tucked up for whipping, it would be an incomparable symphony of black and white, so delectable to the eyes.

Once dressed, I dragged him to the garden. I had ribbons in my hand and he asked what use I intended for them.

Gathering slender branches here and there, by the time Jerome joined me in the shaded depths of the garden, I had in my possession a pliant handful of switches tied with splendid ribbons.

Thinking of
Panty Punishing
Your Husband?

Why not administer his marks after putting him in a pair of our frilly, Sissy Panties? Pull them up, pull them down. Our double-webbed nylon stitching and reinforced cotton crotches will keep them snug and looking new through years of spankings. Ask for our little girl-style bloomers. Great for sessions with the cane or crop!

Sissy Panties

Courtesy WHaP Magazine

A stone seat invited his welcome, it was going to be witness to a scene between schoolgirls.

Seated, I laid my young lover across my knees and, without haste, tucked him up like a big little girl. His white knickers entirely opened, my fingers spread the crack, pushing the shirt up onto his loin. When Jerome's bottom was properly prominent outside the lily-white batiste, I began by making him writhe with a series of full-blooded smacks.

His red bottom contracted, his thighs were criss-crossed by suspenders, he was trembling from the lace of his knickers to the edge of his silk stockings. I made the birch hiss through the air. That produced such a sudden contraction of his behind that it seemed—he not having the ample proportions of the female—to disappear entirely into the feminine whiteness.

Then I pulled down Jerome's knickers completely, from behind, letting the unbuttoned garment fall to the bend of his knees. The tail of his shirt raised with one hand, the other grasping the beribboned haft of my birch, I lashed his posterior rotundities until they contracted and began to bounce.

The hand to begin with, the birch to finish... this was an excellent double whipping that left him with memories—speckles and stripes on his bottom.

This was our game, repeated daily, morning or afternoon. Sometimes the slit of his knickers was simply parted, at other times it was unbuttoned and folded back from behind on his thighs. When I let Jerome have free choice, making him prepare himself, he would unbutton his knickers at the waist before tucking them up himself—in a more feminine way each time. For upright thrashings, especially, with hollowed loins and protruding bottom, he found it distressful enough holding the edges of the skirts to his shoulders, without worrying about the slit that his contortions repeatedly forced to close up again.[4]

One might also note that the main essentials of this strategy may also be applied with equal success to girls:

WHEN THE GOVERNESS considered it necessary to punish a girl, she took her to a room upstairs alone, placed a long soft pillow on a form and made the delinquent lie on it with her legs hanging down on either side. The ankles were then fastened together under the form and the hands in front. She then turned up the girl's clothes to her waist, exposing her just sufficiently for the infliction of a merited punishment, and birched her soundly. When the boy had to be whipped he was made to go upstairs and change his clothes for a punishment dress, which consisted of a short frock and petticoats barely reaching to his knees, stays, chemise and embroidered drawers some inches longer than the frock. The whipping was then inflicted in exactly the same manner as above described, no difference being made between boy and girls in the severity of the whipping; but the boy was sometimes further humiliated by making him remain dressed in his sister's clothes for sometime after the birching. After the first whipping the governess had no difficulty in making any of her pupils submit to their frequent punishments.[5]

REGARDING "A Believer in Discipline"'s question about the best preparation for the rod. I do not think a girl should be whipped when undressed in bed; she should be up, and fully dressed. In fact, she should be required to dress specially for the occasion. It is more humbling, especially for the older girls, to get this baby-discipline when dressed in their best dress, underclothing included, than if they were caught just by accident, as it were, in bed. The only removal of clothing necessary is for the culprit to take off her knickers, which she should be made to do with some ceremony before her chastiser. She should also have to assist as much as possible in her own punishment... by arranging her skirts in such a way as to permit of a free whipping...

In conclusion, no girl I ever heard of would thank anyone for lowering the hem of her under-petticoat after each stroke. After she had felt the first one her only wish would be that the rest would not be so hard, and that they would be soon over.[6]

WE NEVER WORE the open flap drawers which were prescribed in the convent. Ours fit tightly around the thigh and bottom, bordered with pretty lace, tied with ribbons: the front flap folding under the back as customary, the rear flap folding under the belly. A seamstress came tothe house periodically to sew our outer clothing and our underwear. This seamstress was summoned to the house shortly after the step-mother's arrival in order to make drawers and other undergarments for us. My sister had to hold her dress high and try on the drawers so that the step-mother, in the presence of the seamstress, could see how they fit.

After a close examination and testing the step-mother ordered the seamstress to cut the side-slits of the drawers lower by a hand's breadth so that—as she put it—the drawers would not split upon being pulled up or pulled down. We made wholly futile objections against having such large side-slits, but the step-mother was adamant. This episode comes to mind now along with a crystal clear explanation of her design! Obviously the only reason for the large side-slits was that they would enable the step-mother to pull down the rear drawer flap even lower. So at that time the step-mother was already thinking with "love and solicitude" about our bottoms hidden in the drawers and about her birch rod! At that time none of us had been birched and it is probably for this reason that the underlying purpose of the deep side-slits had not occurred to me earlier.

After the introduction of these "practical drawers" one could pull

> down the rear flap to the middle of the thigh once the front slip-knot was loosened. And when dress and blouse were then raised up to the waist, the full bottom lay smooth and bare down to the middle of the thigh—invitingly ready for the rod.[7]

And not only in a domestic or scholastic context: the following is from an account of a judicial caning meted out to a teenage girl in pre-war Singapore (by the British authorities). Once again a special punishing garment is *de rigueur*:

> THE SERGEANT RETURNED a few minutes later holding a length of thin, white material. When she shook this out, I saw it was sewn up into a tube, like all Malay sarongs are made. She held it to my waist, then took a pair of scissors and removed about a half of one thickness, so when it was put around me, skirt-like, it reached near to my calves at the back, while at the front it only reached to the top of my thighs.
>
> Pulling the material even tighter around me, she reached between my legs and grasped the back hem and pulled it up between my legs, pinning it like a nappy, but much tighter. So tight was it over my bottom, I could hardly move my legs.
>
> Finally, I was told to slip the chemise back on, but only the middle button was done up.
>
> She explained, rather disdainfully: "It has been decided that as she is English and the others out there are local, to use a sarong for modesty"—it sounded as if she strongly disapproved of this—"but that thin stuff won't stop her feeling my cane, I assure you. I will take that into consideration!"
>
> This was my first indication that it was she who would be punishing me and that I was for the cane. I looked at her, hoping she would take heed of my misery and pleading expression. Instead of reassurance, I saw a pronounced smirk on her otherwise grim face. I also noted her powerful build.[9]

REGARDING MALES, it is not necessary to go very far down the road of "feminisation"—we might fairly call this "enforced transvestism"—in order to concoct an outfit for the culprit that, by its cut and style, is undeniably a step down this path while at the same time remaining (barely) masculine.

For example, one might use hybrid outfits. These may be as fantastical as you wish, provided they serve their main object, which is to render the unbreeching procedure more agreeable for you and even more diminishing for him. If the clothes are—let us say—difficult to wear at other times, then so much the better for discipline:

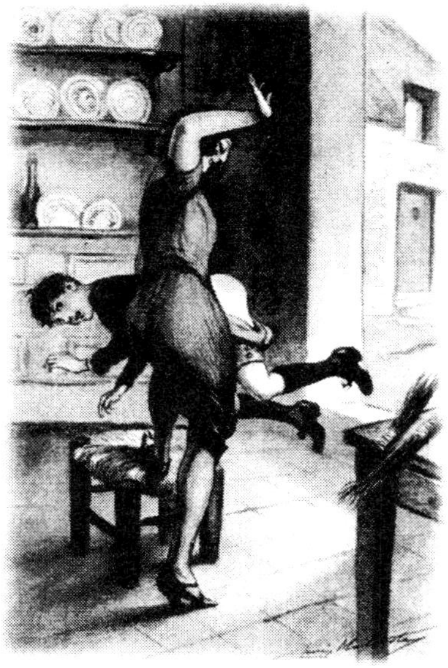

AH, THOSE trousers! They were my masterpiece! I had made all of them myself with extreme care and attention.

Not that I felt obliged to make real boy's clothes. I could buy those easily, or have them made by a dressmaker. I had complete liberty to dress him as I pleased, and without worries about the cost.

But I hadn't wanted to leave to anyone else the task of dressing him in this fashion, showing off the interesting parts of my little slave's pretty body; and in cutting and sewing these little pants I mentally thanked Sister Scolastique who, by means of the Mother Superior's birch-rod, had taught me the proper use of the needle.

Both pairs were of fine white linen striped with pink or blue, and clung tightly to his big boy's bottom (when they hadn't been lowered to mid-thigh) leaving the legs, plump and white, quite bare between the tops of his socks and the band of red or plain blue lace, two fingers wide, with which I bordered the trouser-legs. This lace, encircling his strong thighs, beautifully set off with its rich colours the ivory pallor of his skin.

The jackets with sailor collars which completed this little sensual ensemble did not come lower than the waist where I had fitted them with hidden elastic. Whenever I wished to spank him, having taken down his trousers I had only to push the tail of the shirt underneath this elastic for the entire stomach, thighs and bottom, completely bare, to be accessible...

A few months later (immediately after a spanking in fact) the governess makes a small concession:

> "IN SPITE OF your age you are still only a baby, which is why I am still so often obliged to redden your bottom for you. But your thighs and bottom are now so big that to display them to the world would truly be an immoral act. From now on I shall let you wear longer trousers, at least down to your knees."
>
> "And some long socks also!" he implored, weeping, but I burst out laughing.
>
> "Why not also long socks while you're at it! Has anybody ever seen a villain like you? Already with a burning bottom and wanting to decide the manner in which you're dressed! Take that for your nonsense!"
>
> And two good smacks on his glistening cheeks brought him to order and redoubled his tears.[9]

The above passages have been translated from French and may not be known to many anglophones: but the next must surely be one of the most famous of all:

> HARRIET HAD also taken other measures to ensure her pupil's sense of dependence and inferiority. His schoolboy attire had been exchanged for a costume combining elements of the girlish and the infantile: he now wore a wide-sleeved blouse of white silk, short velveteen trousers, socks and low shoes. This dress, *highly favourable as it was to the infliction of instant discipline* [italics mine], had been devised by Harriet with the principal aim of heightening the boy's self-consciousness in public; and this latter end was so well attained that whenever in the course of their walks together they encountered anyone on the roads and lanes, he was seized by such a fit of shyness and sense of indignity that he would flush and drop his eyes, unable to meet the gaze of persons whom he imagined were looking at him with either amusement or contempt. At such meetings indeed he would feel that not only was his costume observed, but also that the whip of cords which his companion carried with her, unobtrusiveiy doubled in her hand, furnished a further indication of his humiliating servitude. But above all it was other boys of his own age whom he dreaded meeting in these rambles then, noticing the jackets, breeches and boots of these carefree, sturdy youths, seeing the air of joy-

ous freedom with which they roamed over the beautiful wooded countryside, bearing the catapults, fishing-rods and other engines with which the tribe of youth wages a happy and unceasing war on the denizens of pond, tree and meadow—it was then that he would find himself thinking of their liberty with a sharp and wistful envy. They had no governess forever at their side, he thought, their days were not passed in constant subjection to a woman, their waking and sleeping thoughts were not dominated by the menacing image of a cruel whip...[10]

Miss Marwood's pupil Richard Lovell might well have been happy to regain his "schoolboy attire" but for some culprits this very clothing style itself represents a diminution of status. To "juvenise" the male is both a sartorial sanction in its own right and a frequent and logical preliminary to "feminising" him.

The following two remarkable passages on this very subject were submitted to *The Governess* journal in the year 1995. Both contain much food for thought, on this and allied subjects.

WORN FOR PLAY or sport, short trousers are a badge of trendiness; worn under duress, they are a badge of immaturity, of juvenile status, a permanent damper on male arrogance. This can hardly be doubted; and it will be noted with interest by many... that in pre-war Italy, adolescent boys (under 16) were indeed required by law to do so—it was to stop them making use of the brothels!

Our ancestors certainly recognised the sacred importance to the young male of this "rite of passage" from juvenile to adult dress. Then, it was called "breeching"; children of both sexes wore frocks until the age of about five or six; then, little boys were put into their first pair of breeches, often as part of a pleasant family ceremony. That the garment was valued is shewn in William Shenstone's famous seventeenth-century poem *The Schoolmistress*, where he refers to the breeches (which are being taken down in order to facilitate the administration of the birch) as "the stripling's late delight". And it was common practice, when a little (and newly-breeched) boy had been naughty, to put him back into his babyhood frocks for a day or so, to remind him to behave. This must have been a crushing experience. (I believe also that in this custom we have the origins of "petticoating", or putting bad boys into dresses to shame them)

But can this sanction be applied to adult males? I see no reason why not. Miss Kerr-Sutherland herself made bare knees a mandatory condition of dress for all boys (or "boys") who entered her establishment *in statu pupillari.*

Never mind if he looks foolish in such a garment—that, surely, is the point? In fact many younger men do not look at all badly in shorts, provided the cut and material are suitable.

But how to apply the sanction? One must after all be ready with the hated garment for the culprit to put on, and clothes do not grow on trees. They must be acquired, or made, beforehand—I suggest the cutting-down of the trousers of his favourite suit.

Reduced to just above knee-length, and properly taken up and hemmed, they cannot possibly resemble leisure garments and so will convey all the old messages of reduction in status. And he must be ordered to put them on, and to wear them until further notice—you might consider removing or hiding all his long trousers as a further precaution.

If he protests that he has to go to work, reply that no-one is prohibiting him. In the end he must either telephone his employers and take a day off (if financial loss to the family is involved you must make sure it falls where it is deserved); or slink off to work in his garments of humiliation.

Of course, first chance he gets—probably within the hour—he will purchase a pair of "longs"; that is only to be expected. If you suspect this, you must seek them out and confiscate them, not forgetting to bestow a magisterial thrashing as the consequence of direct disobedience.

But if he obeys, and wears the shorts for as long as you bid, you will find, as I have found, that great changes for the better take place in character and deportment. The Magic of Breeches lives on, even in the later 20th century, and all Governesses and disciplinary females should avail themselves of it at every opportunity. There are more ways than one to skin a cat.

I WOULD LIKE to add some personal thoughts to the article by Galla Placidia on the wearing of "shorts" *[above]*. Although I strongly agree in general with that writer, I would wish to take issue with her on some points, and even, if I dare, with one of the ideas expressed by our Patroness.

Firstly let me say that I am of an age to remember short trousers being worn, just above the knee, by boys up to the age of 15 or thereabouts. Long trousers at ten would have been unbelievable! As your correspondent recalls, once a boy had been given his first pair of "longs" he did not, normally, expect ever to wear shorts again.

I believe that, throughout the world, rites of passage are predominantly concerned with the male. This may be because the physical characteristics and expected social behaviour of the adult male differ more markedly from his juvenile counterpart than those of a woman from a girl. Possibly the acquisition of long trousers has formed such a rite because they are also used as a powerful expression of male dominance (consider the expression "wearing the trousers"). In the same way, their removal constitutes an equally powerful expression of submission to higher authority. In my youth boys were often threatened with punishment by use of the words "I'll take your trousers down!" I do not recall girls being told "I'll turn your skirt up" in similar circumstances even though in those days that's what was usually done.

Here is the first point upon which I disagree with Galla Placidia. I do not see short trousers as a sanction or punishment but, like Miss Kerr-Sutherland, as a part of a disciplinary environment. They are a declaration of the wearer's status within the establishment and as such should be worn at all convenient times. For, while punishment is transitory, discipline should be continuous.

I would not normally require a man to go to work in this attire as that would subject him, and indirectly myself, to speculation and comment from people who might not be sympathetic. In the same way he might be permitted to adopt long trousers in the presence of visitors, unless they were acquainted with and approved of the situation. Subject to similar concerns, however, I would expect the wearing of short trousers if he were to go out in company with the mistress of the house.

It is my belief that the general behaviour and attitude of most adolescent males would be considerably improved if their mothers were to impose a similar policy.

In my opinion, cut-down suit trousers will not do as they have an entirely different cut and will almost certainly be of a different material from the grey or navy-blue cloth shorts of the man's childhood. It is still possible to purchase boys' school shorts in adult sizes and an effort should be made to obtain these. They may cost a little more but an appropriate deduction from the recipient's pocket money will produce the added advantage of inhibiting him from the purchase of less suitable forms of clothing.

A word of caution; do not be tempted to purchase short trousers in larger waist sizes, described as "sturdy" under the misapprehension that these will be harder-wearing. In fact, the adjective is intended to apply to the wearer and is a euphemism. They are designed for fat little boys and will probably be unsuitable for an adult.

I am in complete agreement with Galla Placidia that sports-shorts are unacceptable for our purposes and for this reason I tend to avoid the use of the word "shorts". I prefer to call them "short trousers" or, with the justification of history, "knickers" and would insist on the males concerned always referring to the garments in one of these ways.

The one point upon which I differ from the views of our Patroness is in the need for side-buttoning shorts. Since I see the taking down of trousers as an important part of the preparation for punishment which should be thorough and unhurried—to allow both parties to savour the situation to the full—I would expect it to be done before the man is put across his mistress's knee. Should any Full Member wish to apply our Patroness's methods however, it should not be impossible for a competent seamstress to make a pair of side-fastening short trousers, say in black velvet, though nowadays the fastening might well be velcro.

An important advantage, not mentioned by Galla Placidia, of having the male members of your household in short trousers at all times is that the legs of these may be conveniently raised to smack the backs of the thighs whenever "instant" chastisement is needed. This method of punishment is quickly done and will be found to have a beneficial effect out of all proportion to the small effort involved.

To this examination of trousers I would like to add some consideration of what is to be worn under them. Too many women in our society seem to feel that their underwear should be selected to please the men in their lives; men, therefore, who are aware—or are being made aware—of their proper status should have their undergarments specified for them by their womenfolk. Here, there is little need to consider the possibility of embarrassing the man as he will not normally expect anyone to see his underclothes except his mistress and a few trusted guests if his trousers are for any reason removed in front of them.

My own preference in this matter is for white cotton trunks (but most certainly not the modern boxer-shorts. My reasons for preferring this

> choice to briefs are: firstly, I find them easier to pull down. Secondly. they do nothing to pamper the male ego. and thirdly, when a man wearing briefs (under trousers or otherwise) bends over, their hem, running across the centre of the buttocks, spoils the aesthetic appreciation of the sight. Members might also consider emulating one lady of my acquaintance, many years,ago, who, after confiscating and burning all her husband's briefs and making him buy close fitting trunks, embroidered on each pair, in large letters, the words "Property of ——" and her name.[11]

If we are to be perfectly honest, we must admit that both of these worthy lady writers have rather "played down" another cogent reason for dressing up a culprit ridiculously in juvenile attire:

> She made them dress in short pants to transform them into provocative adolescents, though they were already men. The first contact that they had with her was always a reminder of that scene of vigorous whipping with the strap that she had seen administered by her boss to [his son] Georges. The movements had been so deeply registered in her memory that she invariably evoked them: from being unbreeched, to the succession of swift strokes. Sometimes among her lovers there were victims who had not the silent endurance of Georges... She took great pleasure in these punishents, laughing at their entreaties. Because their costumes were like little boys', the whippings she dealt out were with a mixture of birches, straps, and a cane—but her whippings were not whippings for little boys...[12]

Once this motif has been introduced, various hybrids will suggest themselves. One very common one (suggested by the quotation which heads this chapter) is for the subject of your discipline to be made to wear, underneath his everyday trousers, underwear of a markedly different kind to the masculine severity of his outer garments. I understand, and believe, that the mere wearing of such garments may be a valid form of discipline for particularly sensitive males: it is certainly true that to have such apparel revealed through disciplinary unbreeching will force a sudden and sharp exacerbation of any such embarrassment. If witnesses are involved, the shame may become excruciating.

CHAPTER NOTES

1. *Paulette Trahiée* (Jacques D'Icy), Orties Blanches, 1928.
2. *Madame Birchini's Dance*
3. *The Governess Compendium 1993*
4. *Memoires d'une Dominatrice*
5. Letter to *Town Talk*, October 20th, 1883
6. Letter to *Modern Society*, Jan 13, 1900
7. *Confessions & Experiences.*
8. *SR*
9. *Gouvernante et Gouvernée* (Paulette Vergés), Orties Blances, 1931.
10. *Harriet Marwood, Governess*
11. *The Governess Compendium Vol. II*
12. *Memoires d'une Dominatrice*

6: Unusual Unbreechings

Madame Dulaure pushed me onto the bed and removed my skirt... she was sitting on my left and I was partly supported by one of her thighs. What joy! She was going to take my knickers down![1]

SINCE THE variety of ways, modes, settings, environments, ambiences, contexts and other circumstances in which *déculottage* may be executed upon a culprit is beyond computation, this final chapter can do no more than scratch the surface and suggest possibilities to the reader. Commentary is superfluous: let the quoted authorities speak for themselves!

WHEN THE two girls were left alone, Marie advanced towards Isabelle: "Now then, Miss, you heard what your father said... submit yourself... you will have to do so."

"Idiot!" replied the big girl, looking the servant up and down.

"Idiot, that is perhaps your idea, Miss, but nevertheless you are going to receive the whipping."

"You dare touch me! "

"Oh! We will soon see about that." The struggle commenced. Maria threw herself on the young girl and grasped her in her arms, lifting her off the ground and bending her backwards. They both lost their balance.

Isabelle fell on her back, dragging with her Maria, who immediately tried to turn her over in order to lay her on her stomach.

Without uttering a word they continued to struggle: as soon as Maria made her turn half over, Isabelle, quick as lightning, re-established herself in the defensive position destined to protect her buttocks from the degrading fate which menaced them.

The young girl was pale with rage. The servant, on the contrary, was red from the result of the efforts she made.

The contrast between these two girls was as extreme as could be, but at the moment, neither the one nor the other gave a thought to the aesthetics of her attitude. The brunette struggled to defend herself and the other to overcome her.

After several unsuccessful attempts to get Isabelle into position, Maria adopted a brutal stratagem. It had to be accomplished somehow.

Seizing Isabelle's arm vigorously, she began to turn it round. The young girl gave a shriek of pain. She tried to resist. Maria continued the movement and, little by little, Isabelle was obliged to give way to the pressure applied by her torturer.

She lay down on her stomach. Without releasing the arm, Maria took up a leather cushion which had fallen to the ground during the fight, and slipped it under her young mistress's belly, which had the result of bringing into prominence the behind which shaped clearly under the light, thin material of the clinging skirt.

All was ready. With a bound, Maria straddled her victim backwards, her face turned towards the goal she wished to reach; settling her big sit-upon on the young girl's back, she pinned her with all her weight to the carpet.

Isabelle felt that she was beaten. She resigned herself and did not attempt to struggle when she felt the hands pull roughly at her skirt to turn it up.

The drawers were immediately underneath. In order to be thinner, more in the fashion, the young girl was not wearing a petticoat. Maria attacked the frail envelope which covered the condemned parts. She did not take the trouble to open the slit, but proceeded to remove the drawers entirely.

First of all she unhurriedly piled the skirt over the loins, then she searched round the waist for the string of the drawers. When she found it she untied it carefully, then slipped the dainty drawers along the thighs. She next lifted up the chemise and looked at the little plump bottom, with its deep crease, almost a boy's bottom, rather more rounded though, with a bold line that gave it an impudent air.

The white silk stockings and same coloured garters set off admirably the dull golden skin of the lovely brunette. The cushion placed under the belly threw up the bottom which opened out, emphasising its furrow of warm shade, proffering itself in its most favourable amplitude to the thorough spanking which it was fated to receive:

"Look out, my beauty, I'm beginning..."[2]

THE HONOUR (or burden) of ceremonially baring Teddy Pearson's bottom for punishment—probably the moment of supreme humiliation for the big lad—had freely been bestowed on Sally Grainger, who had suffered more than any at the victim's hands.

Sally, who had no brothers, and had indeed never seen a male backside, had been diffident, until Coral had said: "Sally, he pulled up your skirt. The least you can do for your honour is pull down his pants. Personally, I call it a just revenge"—and Sally had been unable to fault this ruthless logic.

She now stepped forward and grasped each leg-hem. She pulled gingerly downwards. The football shorts slid slowly over Teddy's hips and began their inexorable descent.

At this moment he changed his tune.

"Please!" he said, quavering. "Don't!"

The terror in his voice struck a new note in the hearts of all the girls—who, after all, were decent British maidens with no more than the usual proportion of inherent human cruelty. Sally hesitated. Belinda, who was kind to dumb animals, felt her heart quail in pity. Marjorie, who had already brought severe humiliation upon him—and injured his knee withal—looked at Coral in sudden doubt. But Heather, who had been brought up with five boisterous boys, had seen them physically punished time and time again in a no less degrading manner (and who had suffered more than one such punishment herself), maintained a stone face. Felicity, who had received one searing birch-stroke across her own bottom and was, perhaps understandably, keen to see the same effect wrought upon another bottom, said nothing but looked expectantly at Coral; and Coral herself, though she too was affected by the genuine ring of terror in Teddy's voice, knew that it was for this moment that they had laboured so hard, and for which all the planning had been carried through. As the eldest, and perhaps wisest, she also realised that this sudden submission might well be no more than a ploy, and that were it to be heeded Teddy would remain unpunished and unchecked. That at least could not be borne. She hardened her heart and nodded abruptly to Sally.

The shorts slid down to Teddy's knees. There was a collective sigh from those assembled, and a wail of despair from Teddy. Sally stood back, contemplating her handiwork.

Coral said: "Now your disgrace is complete!"[3]

This being done, the Boy was tasked
Still lacking Breeches, for to aske
My Lady's Maid to help him searche
The Wood for Twigges to make a Birch.
Meanwhyle for Amarantha and
Fair Jocasta, with her own Hand
My Lady prepar'd fine Sweetmeates
And Drinkes to Sip whyle he was beate.

Some little Tyme did pass until
The Boy return'd, and with him stille
The Maid, one Julia by Name
Who carried Ribbonnes: he, in Shame
A Bunch of Twigges but freshlie cutte

And there, the Maid around their Butt
Did tye these Ribbonnes skilfullie
To make a Rod, then presentlie
Having swung it through the Aire
Some several Tymes, pronounced it Fair
And handed it respectfullie
With lower'd Head to her Lady
Then made to leave. Nay! Go not yet
For one more Taske that I shall sette
Shall you performe. Before he's Whipp't
This Youth you see must firste be stripp't
Of all his Cloathes: and then shall you
Across this Bench before the view
Of these young Ladies bend him o'er
And use the cords within this Drawer
To tye his limbes most carefullie
That he may not by Force break free
For such Constraint, I do believe
He'll need to bear what he'll receive.4

AFTER THE USUAL salutations, talk about the weather, and an enquiry of the Doctor, "whether he had had sufficient exercise in school this damp day; "to which the sage replied, "only fifteen, and two of them babies;" we entered the dining-room. It was a spacious apartment, and looking round, I saw that, besides the lights on the table, there were four candelabras in the corners of the room, which appeared to be held up by four boys, with their faces to the wall, their trousers down to their heels, and their shirts pinned up to their shoulders. I never saw four chubbier or whiter bottoms. On a nearer inspection it was seen that their hands were so fastened as to give them the appearance of holding up the candles. As the master of the house made no remark on these singular pieces of furniture, and the servants took no notice except pricking them with a fork as they passed, we guests said nothing...The conversation continued on ancient sculpture, and when the first course was removed, our host said, "I am desirous to colour these statues of mine bright red, if these gentlemen will help me," and the servant presented each of us with a long, springy rod, decked with a hundred buds... For some time no sound was heard but the swishing of the twigs, and the roaring of the twigged...

Nothing remarkable occurred until dessert, when four small plates were placed at the corners of the table, which were occupied by four charming boys of twelve or thirteen, dressed in light-blue jackets trimmed with silver-braid and very tight white trousers. These Acolytes or Ganymedes, or whatever you please, handed round the fruit, cake and wine, and cherfully partook of the portions given to them. I saw them, however, eye with anxiety a long pasteboard box at the end of the table, which our host now opened, saying, "These are the sweetmeats for which my housekeeper is justly famous," and took out four small rods, tied-up with blue riband...They were over our knees in a trice: we smacked the tight white trousers for some time in an Epicurean way, before we untrussed them, while the salacious Doctor could not stand the covering for a moment, and, setting to with the rod, had worked it to a stump, while we were still enjoying the urchins' struggles...[5]

BETTY BROWN, THE girl to be whipped, was ordered to stand out, which she did, looking very shamefaced. She was a big, tall girl in appearance, far more robust than either the Lady Maria or her cousin. She was going to be still-room maid at Lord Royston's, a fine house in the next county, for she was a clever girl, though careless and troublesome at times.

Betty stood before the party, till Miss Thomas, the schoolmistress, rose, and curtseying, read out the punishment. "Betty Brown will fetch the rod," my lady said; and the girl went, colouring crimson, and ready to cry. When she came back, she knelt, and presented it, as was the fashion, and then Mademoiselle said sharply—"Kiss it." That was one of the new notions she had brought from France, and we didn't like it— we never had to do it before she came.

Betty kissed it, looking dreadfully terrified while she was prepared for flogging. Joan stripped her, and she was made to fold up her clothes, one by one, as though she were going to bed, while we all sat in our places looking on, not allowed to move or speak. When she stood ready for the rod, the bell was rung for the dairywoman—a great, stout person, who had the enviable task of horsing us when we were birched.[6]

THESE NOCTURNAL maraudings had their dangers, as the mistresses would frequently make their rounds. But the danger was an attraction. For—shall I confess it?—while we feared the whip, we grew to desire it.

Fig. 9: Unbreeching Under Third Party Restraint

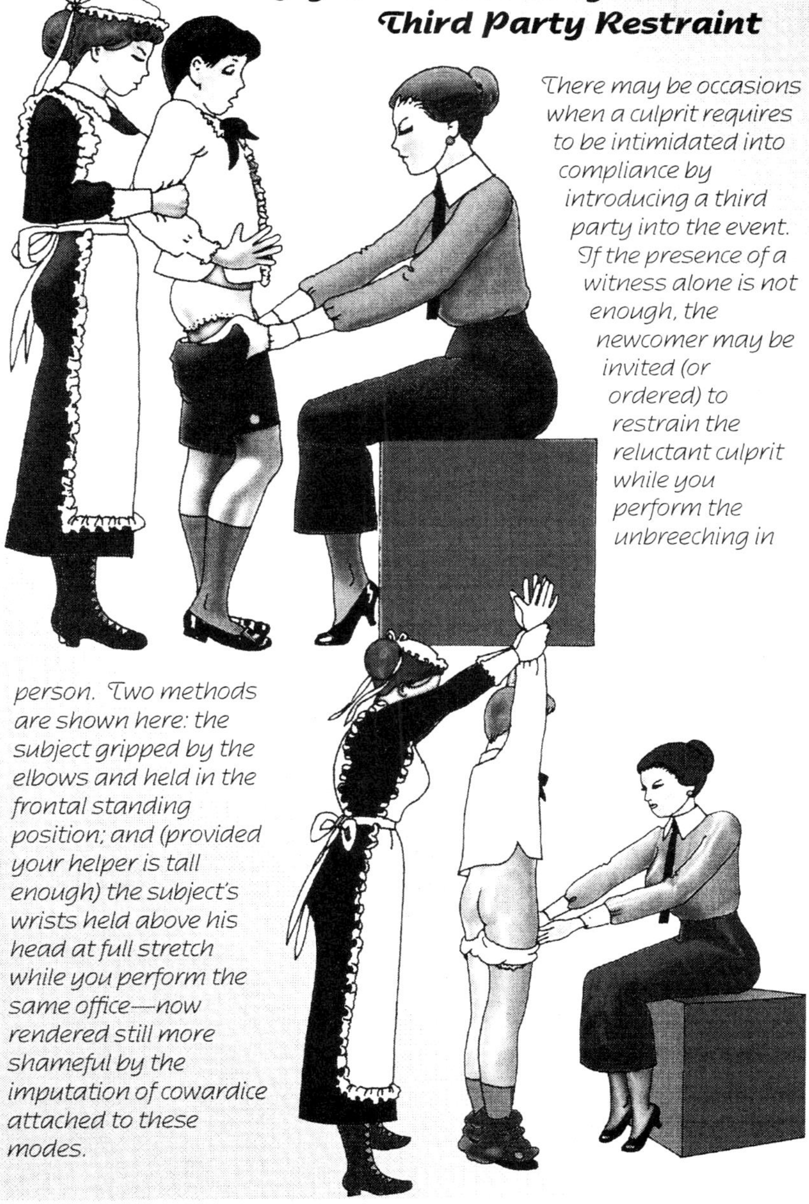

There may be occasions when a culprit requires to be intimidated into compliance by introducing a third party into the event. If the presence of a witness alone is not enough, the newcomer may be invited (or ordered) to restrain the reluctant culprit while you perform the unbreeching in person. Two methods are shown here: the subject gripped by the elbows and held in the frontal standing position; and (provided your helper is tall enough) the subject's wrists held above his head at full stretch while you perform the same office—now rendered still more shameful by the imputation of cowardice attached to these modes.

On certain days, whether because the weather was heavy or stormy, or for some other inexplicable reason, we would grow restless and commit faults with the obvious and sole object of being whipped. Sometimes Lady Flayskin, Stella, and all the mistresses were not numerous enough for the flogging which was required—our desires in this direction being always gratified to the best of the abilities of our superiors. At these times, six boys and perhaps ten girls would be ranged in a kneeling line with drawers down, awaiting the penance of the birch.

What a chorus of cries, entreaties, sobs and wails would then be heard! If the thick walls and the large garden had not deadened these sounds, an astonished passer-by would certainly have thought they proceeded from a madhouse. For never, unless the recollection of early days, similarly passed, had come to him, could he have guessed the truth.[7]

ALL AT ONCE there was a roll of drums, the lights on the stage changed to a deep rose, and a drop-curtain swept aside, revealing two statuesque female figures in long white gowns, who had been watching. A wild arpeggio from the harp, like the susurrus of an autumn wind, succeeded, and the chorus of children, wailing, shrank back in a calculated disarray towards the wings; then the Matrons advanced slowly, to a solemn, throbbing pizzicato of bass viols.

Their appearance was truly wonderful. With faces painted dead white, mounting false chins and noses which almost met over tiny mouths, their foreheads graced with rows of curls like inverted question marks, and wearing enormous mob-caps which quivered and swayed upon their heads, they moved slowly upstage, nodding portentously and making gestures of outrage. A round of applause greeted them, for these were Mrs Bowyer and Mrs Barker.

And now the former took a striking attitude, the harp sounded a few notes, and she delivered a glorious recitative, her majestic contralto filling the theatre as she expressed her indignation and horror, her well-nigh disbelief in the testimony of her eyes, while she clasped her hands, raised them in the air and dropped them to her sides, rolling her eyes and shaking her head; an occasional interpolation from Mrs Barker's golden soprano cut across her words, and then the two voices joined in a sombre and stirring duet in which execrations were mingled with promises of punishment and invocations to the spirit of birch.

The duet ended with three long notes in alt, uttered by the Matrons in unison. This was the call to the servants, and as the applause of the audience reached its climax four strapping girls carrying rods rushed on to the stage. Now, as the orchestra struck up a jolly bourrée, to whose accented rhythm was executed a short and lively bacchanale, the orphans retreating and fleeing, the servant girls pursuing, grasping, and losing; cries of alarm, triumph, and vexation mingled with the invigorating music, the dance became a wild rout of flying forms, a whirling kaleidoscope of smock and sash, of bare limb and lacy pantalette, from which at last two of the serving wenches emerged, each with an orphan securely horsed on her back, and the music ceased with a plangent clash of cymbals.

To the sounds of an exquisite solo by the premier violin, the two captives, a boy and a girl, werte now lovingly and ceremoniously untrussed. Ah, what a delightful operation this was! What ravishing contours were exposed, what quiverings, what tremblings and trepidations, what rosy reluctancies, as the plump fesses emerged and the two dear children were prepared for the neat birch rods in the hands of Bowyer and Barker!

Then all was quiet; the tableau arranged itself, each captive flanked by Matron and domestic, the remaining children creeping close as at the bidding of fear and fascination, and Mrs Barker, her rod upraised, began to deliver a thrilling lecture full of the old-fashioned phrases of nursery eloquence. By degrees her emotion mounted, as if like an Homeric hero she were exciting herself by her own threats and vauntings; her voice rose, throbbing and fulminating in sombre crescendi, her arm gesturing with motions ever more purposeful, until at last, as a superb and stately period rolled to its close, the twigs descended with a rich and urgent hiss and the flagellation commenced to a softly resumed music.[8]

THERE WAS NO longer any trace of the gay, light-hearted, wilful socialite who had picked Pepin up, as it were, at the Barbican, selecting him on a whim like any other not-too-expensive purchase. The sleepy petulance of the morning hours had quite disappeared. All the Duchess Honoria Eugenia's exalted bloodline was flowing strongly in her veins: she exuded the deadliness of aspect of the feudal seigneur who, having successfully put down a local jacquerie and captured the ringleaders, is now able to devote considerable, pleasant ingenuity to devising the most horrifying means of capital retribution in his power.

"Go to my lady Berthe," she said, "and ask her in my name to be kind enough to untie your points for you, since you have plainly forgotten how! Address her as *Tante* Berthe and remember to say please like a good little boy." There was a delighted, appreciative snigger from Alicia Renata, and open smiles from the other ladies. Palms were placed across mouths, glances and whispers exchanged. Her Grace's countenance remained unmoved.

With burning countenance Pepin shuffled over to Berthe's chair. She eyed him with amused disdain. He said, choking: "*Tante* Berthe, her Grace commands me to ask you to be kind enough to... please... to let down my hose."

The ladies laughed, but the Duchess was not satisfied. "That is not what I told you to say. Say it properly! Stay your hand, Berthe, I must have him word-perfect."

Confused, Pepin stumbled through the humiliating little speech a second time.

"You do not desire Berthe to let down your hose. You wish her only to unfasten your points, and so you were instructed," said the Duchess sharply. Thus apprised of the invalid phraseology, the wretched Pepin stuttered out the dreadful sentence a third time. Then—since his tormentrix proclaimed herself dissatisfied with his general diction—a fourth. The Duchess nodded, reluctantly, and her tirewoman leaned forward and, with ladylike neatness and precision, lifted the front of the surcoat and unknotted the two cloth points. They fell loose, like beheaded serpents: the hose slithered from Pepin's hipbone and sagged in folds around his pelvis, buttocks and thighs, held in place by surface tension, good tailoring and frantic thigh-pressure exerted by Pepin. Berthe released the surcoat and leaned back, placidly examining her victim with a half-smile. Her victim stood there, knock-kneed and trembling.

"Now go to my lady Kristina and ask her—politely, remember!—to pull your hose down to your knees. Call her *Tante* Kristina. And when you have done that you may go to 'Tante' Winfrida and ask her to tie your points tightly at your knees so that you do not kick like a little boy

Fig. 10: Public Unbreeching

If there is anything more shaming to a culprit than to be unbreeched, it is to suffer this fate in the presence of witnesses (of the opposite sex, preferably). It is likely that some prior planning may be involved if such an event is to be stage-managed effectively, but all the same do not hesitate, if necessary and appropriate, to "seize the moment"!

when I punish you over my lap."

Alicia Renata clapped her hands, the ladies guffawed and Pepin blushed, if possible, an even deeper shade of crimson than before.

"A boon, cousin!" pleaded Alicia Renata. "A boon! Cede Kristina's task to me!"

The Duchess nodded assent, my lady Kristina (who had been leaning forwards eagerly) settled back, pouting with disappointment; and Pepin began to shuffle, with bowed head, hunched shoulders, knock knees and drooping hose, towards his youthful Nemesis, whose green eyes were alight with pleasure, and whose slender, white fingers were already crooked, flexing forwards to advance his disgrace by the designated increment.

The fingers lightly grasped the loose waist-folds of the hose and, after a luxurious pause when Alicia Renata's green eyes appeared to close for an moment, began to slide them slowly downwards. There was complete silence in the chamber.

"Look at me!" she said, softly. "Look. At. Me."

Pepin raised his swimming eyes to meet hers. They were dancing with life, twin pools of elvish delight that gleamed with satisfaction, cruel enjoyment—and, perhaps, something else. Slowly, deliberately, working with small, efficient, unhurried movements, she eased the rumpled, yellow-and-black garment down Pepin's thighs. Then, encroaching in her enthusiasm on my lady Winfrida's preserves, she proceeded to knot the points at the knees, once, twice, pulling the mass of knots malevolently tight.

"*Tante* Alicia must take his breeches down, and send him to *mutti* to have his bottom smacked," she commented lightly.

This gruesome speech might shrivel anyone to whom it was addressed under similar circumstances, and Pepin was duly shrivelled, but it was Alicia Renata's specific use of the word *breeches* which suddenly and poignantly recalled for him all his exploded dreams and aspirations, his ridiculously romantic fancies, his absurd, ludicrous, failed ambitions—all symbolised by his lost breeches. Pepin burst into tears and buried his face in his hands.[9]

CHAPTER NOTES

1. *Paulette Trahiée*
2. *Sweet Sixteen*
3. "The Vigilantes of Durnley Parva" (*QoG*)
4. "Amarantha" (*SR*)
5. "The Doctor's Little Dinner" from *Venus School-Mistress*
6. *An Illustrated History of the Rod*
7. *Stays & Laces*
8. *Venus and Tannhauser (Under the Hill)* by Aubrey Beardsley. Some sources claim that this passage was "added" many years afterwards by the Canadian disciplinary writer and pasticheur John Glassco (as "Miles Underwood" author of *Harriet Marwood, Governess)*.
9. From "The Lost Breeches" by Louise Malatesta (*The Governess*, Issue XII)

More Exquisite Disciplinary Literature from AKS Books

The Wand of Venus:
The High History of the Birch Rod

The Birch Rod is the most ancient, renowned, elegant, poignant, romantic and beautiful of all instruments of physical correction, and once was the very symbol of refined corporal punishment in its most classic form. In modern times, however, it has fallen out of fashion, while the secrets of its manufacture—and knowledge of the variety of ways a well-made rod may be put to satisfactory use—are rapidly being lost forever. *The Wand of Venus* is a dazzling and erudite compendium of birchen lore, compiled from a huge variety of expert sources from classical times to the present day. Histories, anecdotes, eulogies, factual accounts, recommended procedures and other Arcana of the Rod, intriguingly assembled and beautifully presented with over 80 rare and original illustrations.

The Queen of the Grove

First published in 1993 to international acclaim, Louise Malatesta's classic collection of stories and poems celebrating the Disciplinary Female, exquisitely illustrated throughout by Sardax, recaptures the literary, artistic and production standards of the 'Golden Age' (1920-35) of Disciplinary Fiction. This superb volume is truly in a class of its own.

The Fellowship of the Rod

The longest (four volumes) and most ambitious novel ever created in the Disciplinary genre, a journey of the imagination spanning three continents, two centuries and a dozen generations. Its subject is a strange inheritance—the passion for physical discipline—which becomes an obsession for each individual to whom the torch passes...